NERO

BOOK 2:
THE MUMMY STRIKES

Christofer Nigro

Cover Logo Design and Formatting by Elden Ardiente of Lungga Creatives

DEDICATION

This one is all for my beloved grandmother Gertrude "Trudie" Nigro, whom I was blessed to have as my grandmother, best friend, and fellow fan of scary movies, kaiju, giant robots, superheroes, and pulp fiction for such a long swath of my journey through life. I also thank the God and Goddess every day that she lived to be 95, and that our family had her with us for so long.

Trudie, I will never stop trying to make you proud, and the stuffed bunny you thoughtfully got me as a gift one Easter will always keep me company on my office desk.

Author's Note: Matters of Perspective

For this second installment of Mike Nero's saga, I believe a few words of explanation are in order to you, my valued readers, about some of the aesthetic choices I made, and why I did so.

This book will feature the initially independent but ultimately intertwining stories of not only Mike Nero, teen werewolf, but also Walter Lavelle, our titular mummy character (to see how this young man gains control over such a creature, simply start reading the book after this explanatory note!). These aesthetic decisions, which I hope the readers will find interesting, were designed to both allay confusion between scenes, let us know which of the two titular characters a given story scene was focused upon (if either), and also to pay homage to the horror comics of yesteryear that greatly inspired this tale (and much of my writing in the genre, for that matter).

So, here is how the story will be told.

Scenes focusing on Mike Nero will be preceded by a wolf head symbol, and like the first book, will be told in the first person/past tense by Nero himself.

Scenes focusing on our titular mummy will be preceded by the emblem of a mummy's sarcophagus and will be told from a second person/present tense POV just as the writers of the narration captions of stories from the great horror comics published during the 1960s and '70s – whether by Marvel, DC, or Warren etc. – seemed to have a notable preference for. There was just something about the mood evoked by this way of telling a horror story that really caught on with the authors of the comic book medium of that era – whether it was an issue of Marvel's *Werewolf by Night* or *Tales of the Zombie*; or, Warren's *Creepy* or *Eerie*; or, DC's *House of Mystery* or *Swamp Thing*, et al. – this was a popular way of telling such stories in that medium, and this nostalgic nod with the scenes focusing on our mummy character will invoke those halcyon days of terror tale telling.

Scenes featuring both Nero *and* our mummy character will be preceded by both the wolf *and* sarcophagus symbols and will likewise be told in the first person/past tense by Nero, since he is, after all, the main character of this series. Hence, his perspective will be the favored one in such cases.

Finally, story scenes featuring neither our werewolf or mummy characters will be demarcated by the usual trio of asterisks and will be told from a third person/past tense perspective. This simply made sense to me since Nero was not around to witness or recall such events, and there was no mummy present to unite his perspective with that of the reader (as is the case in narration from a second person POV).

For those who are discovering Nero's story for the first time with this book, welcome to the saga, and be sure to pick up *Nero Book 1: The Beast Emerges* (still on sale via Amazon) for the beginning! And for those of you who have already read the first volume, welcome *back* to the saga, and I hope you will enjoy this second outing of Nero as much as you hopefully did the first!

Christofer Nigro

NERO

BOOK 2:
THE MUMMY STRIKES

Buffalo, New York, early December 1981

A young couple sat cuddled together in front of a spread of bushes, bundled up for the cold, snowy weather but enjoying the warmth emanating from not only a small bonfire they had burning – but from each other's arms.

I really envied that guy as I rushed towards the couple silently on all fours in my werewolf form. My muzzle opened wide and slavering as I rapidly moved in the happy twosome's direction without their knowledge, the animal side of me largely in control and eager to satiate its urge to hunt. It was a compulsion I had to periodically let the lycanthrope out to satisfy, lest it overwhelm my human persona. The unwitting pair held each other and stared blissfully at a multi-color light display in commemoration of the Christmas season.

My approach was so quiet, and their attention so caught up in the admiration of each other and the blinking lights, they had no hope of noticing me before my bulky, hirsute gray form crashed through the shrubbery directly behind them. They screamed in unison, drowning out my gruff canine snarls as their thick winter coats were spattered with rivulets of blood.

My scarlet-flecked muzzle rose from out of the bushes to reveal its many razor-sharp teeth and incredible jaw strength crushing the life out of a captured raccoon. The terrified young couple covered their faces as streams of blood from the perforated animal continued to spurt onto their upper bodies. Yes, for a quick moment they had thought the blood was their own.

The girl leaped to her feet screaming, "Oh my god1 Oh my god! Oh my god…!"

The young man did the same and yelled, "Holy shit! I think it's the fucking wolfman!"

No, I wasn't going after them… I had not ceded that amount of control to the animal side this night. My ultra-keen hearing, sense of smell, and ability to see heat patterns in the dark had detected the presence of the raccoon hiding in the bushes behind those two. They simply happened to pick that particular spot to create their fire-heated cuddle nest. A bad choice on their part, considering there was a raccoon in those bushes. Ha.

The horrified duo rushed into the safety of a house a few doors down. I was too busy tearing the crumpled body of the porky little animal to pieces to be overly concerned with their flight and terror. It was only after my hunt-lust was satisfied that I began to feel a bit bad for scaring the shit out of those two – and quite literally in the case of one of them, considering the nature of the stench they left behind that my lupine nostrils could easily detect.

As soon as I finished my fur-covered entree, I dashed across the street and behind various tall bushes and parked vehicles in a grayish blur of motion. My wolf-enhanced mind became quite adept at building a detailed mental map of the Queen City's geography, much as real wolves and bears do of their woodland environs, and I could cover several miles in a remarkably short time.

The endurance I displayed in my lupine form was every bit as astonishing as my strength and speed, so this was rarely any trouble. My biggest concern was running into Buffalo's gun-wielding finest, who were now on the look-out for me despite my helping them end the menace of the Jack Dog and his pack of bloodthirsty canines last month.

I could hardly blame them, to be fair. The fact is, I had not taken on the power of the wolf for altruistic reasons, and I was a young boy with a formidable weapon on a mission of revenge.

Which led to two other concerns of mine: who the next target on my shit list would be; and the issue of my peers catching on to the fact that the now much-feared West Side Wolf Man was actually me. Especially since said werewolf was tearing into a bunch of *them*. Not that those assholes didn't deserve it, mind you. But I obviously couldn't expect them to agree with me on that.

Your name is Walter Lavelle, and you are thankful that your uncle, who is a Buffalo councilman, was able to get you that internship at the Buffalo Museum of Antiquities. You have always had a fascination with the mysteries of ancient Egypt, especially their rigorous attempts to understand and circumvent the death process. You studied their practices in depth for years of your young life in the hope that you may one day figure out a way to recreate and even perfect those processes (which far too often came with a hefty price tag even when they were successful.) It is a grandiose dream on your part, Walter; but it is a dream a lonely and alienated seventeen-year-old who seeks a way out of his hated and humble station in life cannot help but obsess over.

Of course, you are also very fascinated with the pharaohs and the power they wielded over what was perhaps the greatest human civilization to rise in the ancient world. Power is something you have always been without in the Western society of the 20th century that you call home, and you long for a taste of it. Your fondest desire is to acquire your share of the power that the world has to offer, and to use it to right the many injustices and indignities you have been forced to endure.

You are reminded of these infractions against your dignity every time you look in the mirror and see the lack of attractiveness, athletic aptitude, and natural charm that is your lot to bear. The image that looks back at you is a mousy, bespectacled, and lanky African American with frizzy hair and a highly imperfect complexion that is your constant reality.

This has made you the target of numerous jokes and to be avoided by every girl you have ever desired, thus forcing your relationships with them to be limited to elaborate but empty fantasies. You are certain that the pharaohs never had to endure this. Sitting on their golden thrones, they were the undisputed masters of all they surveyed. They were considered to be gods on Earth whose mere words determined the fate of every citizen who served and labored for them. How you have always longed for that kind of life, Walter Lavelle! You believe the world owes you that much for all it has deprived you of for seventeen years now.

Once you heard of the much-belabored Egyptian exhibit that would be coming to the museum, you all but begged your uncle to get you an internship there. You explained your passion with this ancient civilization, your hard-earned knowledge acquired due to countless hours of intensive study; you pleaded that the extra credits you would earn could be a boon to the college education that you would begin in the Fall of '82.

"Are you sure you're up to this, Walt?" your Uncle Maurice asked you in that tone you hated. "I mean, it's a lot of work, kid. And a lot of responsibility. This exhibit will feature the real preserved mummy of the Pharaoh Nebka from Egypt's 4th Dynasty. It's also gonna have a lot of relics from the high priests that served him. It's an expensive display that'll require a lot of knowledge of the subject."

"I know that, Uncle Maurice," you replied, trying to keep a respectful tone. "But I've spent my whole life studying Egypt. So, I'm pretty sure that I know as much about Nebka as anyone else you could hire. Like, I know that he was king for a very short reign because his corruption caused his own priests to turn on him and carry out a seriously harsh punishment. I can really do a good job showing off the exhibit to the visitors."

"Yeah, Walt, I read the history myself, but understand that all the info we have is fragmentary and impossible to fully verify. Be sure to make that clear so you do not spout any inaccuracies that a knowledgeable visitor might catch you on. That would make you look stupid, and me as well for giving you the position."

You pouted but kept your cool, as it was still important to humble yourself to this man who held *your* fate in his hands. Yes, just like a pharaoh did with the multitudes beneath them. How you longed to reverse that relationship you have with your uncle, as well as everyone else in your life.

"Okay… I hear you, Unc. I won't mess up. This is very important to me. I'll go over every text I have again. I'll re-read every one of those scroll copies I collected. I'll get everything right, I promise."

"Yeah, okay, that sounds like a good idea, Walt. In the meantime, I'll talk to the curator and see what I can do."

As promised, you revisited all your books and scrolls describing the wonders of that ancient civilization of the black sands. It was no problem on your part, as your obsessive interest in Egyptology would likely have caused you to spend your spare time between your regular studies reading about that ancient civilization anyway. And it was not as if you had much of a social life to speak of, correct?

Your particular interest in the funerary traditions of the kings and the mummification process caused you to believe that you had established a strong subliminal connection with the dreaded Egyptian deity Anubis, the jackal-headed god who presided over all matters concerning death and burial rites. You have recently felt this rapport stronger than ever before, and you're learning of the exhibit coming to the Buffalo Museum seemed like it was more than just a coincidence.

The week passes swiftly, Walter. Your uncle came through for you, as you had hoped. Hence, you now find yourself enthusiastically discussing the Nebka exhibit with a group of visiting professors from the college you plan to attend next year. Along with them are a group of seniors from various local high schools who also sought early college credits by taking advantage of the museum's program, which is using this exhibit to provide a quick study course on Egyptology.

You not only want to impress these professors, but also a certain girl named Kendra Calloway, a bright and attractive high school junior from your neighborhood who had caught your eye more than once. You do your utmost to sound as brilliant and informative as possible while trying not to get "tongue-tied" in her presence… and to avoid displaying your anger at how close she seemed to stick to Vance Jacobs. He was a popular, athletic, and handsome student from your own school, someone whose position in life you longed for. Standing alongside Vance was his friend and frequent partner-in-crime, Edwin Tanner.

"Nebka of the 4th Dynasty was a fascinating fella," you explain to the small crowd with some enthusiasm. "Really, he was! His brief reign was so full of corruption that some of the deciphered scrolls allege that his own high priests drugged him and had him subjected to a really nasty punishment. It was a penalty that some mystically adept members of the priesthood concocted for certain individuals they wanted to punish as harshly as possible: they bandaged up the body of King Nebka and subjected him to a slow death via the poisonous embalming procedure. But, and here is the real kicker…"

You look at the audience in front of you and beam widely, hoping you can pique their excitement with what was coming next in your spiel. It requires all the willpower you possess not to frown when you notice Vance whisper something to Kendra that causes her to look at you and giggle derisively.

Damn it! Am I overdoing things here and coming off as a nerd?

You bite your tongue and continue your speech, realizing that you must soldier on with the lecture.

"Well, the kicker was this. The priests supposedly performed a mystical rite of penance that trapped the evil victim's soul in their dead body, so they could never pass on to the afterlife and be properly judged by Osiris. So, yeah, they would be stuck in that decaying but preserved body of theirs for eternity, which would then be entombed. It was believed they would experience at least intermittent bouts of full conscious awareness during that incredible span of time. This horrible punishment was supposedly done to several during the various dynasties, including two evil high priests known as Imhotep, and a slave of the Swarili tribe who was punished in this way for leading an unsuccessful rebellion…"

"Is all of this really true, young man?" Doctor Kent Billington, a professor of archeology at the Elmwood University of Buffalo, suddenly interrupted.

You glare at the man with confusion. "Huh?"

"I mean, I have heard similar rumors," Billington continued, "but it always came off as a bunch of fantastical chicanery to me. What were your sources for this?"

"Well," you reply with a slight stammer, "mention of this is made in the *Scroll of Nephrus* and the *Book of Anubis,* both of which contain passages which say…"

"Then that explains it!" Billington interjects. "Those have long been considered suspect sources written by ancient charlatans. None of them are viewed as legitimate texts by serious archeologists and Egyptologists of the modern age."

You grit your teeth hard upon seeing Vance quietly say, "Oh, man," followed by smirks and giggles from Edwin, Kendra, and a few other students.

"Well, sir, professional opinions and scholarship varies on that," you add in an attempt to salvage your lecture.

"I'm sorry, young man, but the consensus for decades now has been that those sources are utter poopycock."

You notice how he made a point to pronounce the word as "*poopy*cock" rather than the proper "poppycock," which elicits yet more derisive giggles from Kendra and her party.

"He said '*poopy*cock,'" you heard Vance snigger. "That was cold, man."

"Look," you mutter with a nervous splutter, "I can show you some good evidence on the next and best little gem we have here in this exhibit. See that sarcophagus? The actual mummified body of Nebka is in there, whose tomb was recently discovered and unearthed by the Carnahan Society. Check it out."

You walk over to the gleaming sarcophagus and pull open its ornately decorated lid, exposing the exceedingly tall body of Nebka. The ancient cadaver is wrapped thoroughly in a few layers of dirty, tattered bandages, though his brownish, horribly withered face is exposed. His arms are positioned over his chest in a criss-cross pattern, something commonly done with male mummies.

You hope that the audience will be awed by the sight, but instead you hear only groans of revulsion. Kendra blatantly recoils from the combination of seeing the body and whiffing the rank odor that emanates from the opened stone casket. Dr. Billington simply glowers at you and the mummy with a perplexed countenance.

"See, look at that!" you say with the clear expectation of impressing the audience.

"Geez, can't they spray that thing with Lysol or something?" Vance utters just loud enough for you to hear him. Kendra was still looking too revolted to laugh at or appreciate the jape.

"I am looking," the university teacher replies, "and smelling, as well. King Nebka looks quite dead to me, with no sign that his soul is trapped in there. It's all just puerile superstition."

"But that isn't the evidence I was referring to," you note with a hint of urgency. "That can be found on the inscriptions etched onto the sarcophagus." You point with a shaking finger at the colorful hieroglyphs painted onto the stone to emphasize where to look. "See those birds with human heads in flight? They represent the *Ba,* the 'outer' or etheric shell that encapsulates the spirit, which is distinct from the *Ka,* the 'inner' or truly astral part of the soul that goes off to the *Duat* – that is, the Egyptian conception of the afterlife – for judgment by Osiris upon death.

"But see how that bird in front of the character for 'tomb' is bound rather than flying? That suggests the *Ba* is trapped inside the dead body. As a result, the etheric shell will not dissipate to release the *Ka* as it ordinarily does following death to enable it to leave the mortal coil and journey to the other side."

Billington shakes his head with a scornful smile. "I have studied hieroglyphs for many years and never have I seen a bound bird character before."

You now begin sounding visibly flustered. "Because that symbol is the equivalent of ancient mystical jargon! It represents a cruel but rare procedure that doesn't appear often in Egyptian scrolls or etchings…"

"Alright," Billington abruptly says to his study group," we should move on now to the other exhibits before our time is up. Thank you for that lecture, young man. Just remember what I said about using legit sources next time."

The professor leads his group of students away from the Nebka exhibit, and you see Vance briefly turn and shake his head at you before they leave your wing of the museum. You clench your fists in rage, wishing you could pummel both he and Billington to a bloody pulp.

With that, you resolve to stay overnight and study the scrolls and artifacts that came with the exhibit. You are determined to find a way to tap into the power that this brutal but undeniably powerful pharaoh once enjoyed.

At long last, you would find a way to *make* these people respect you if they refused to offer it to you freely, Walter. As a result, Kendra would finally notice you in a positive way, while the likes of Billington, Vance, and their cronies would fear you. Their lives would continue or not depending on your good graces, on your slightest whim.

Little were you aware that your midnight studies would bear fruit of a most terrifying nature for the entire Queen City. And you were likewise unaware that its acquisition would set you on a brutal collision course with another young man in a similar situation.

***

A sullen Officer Lamar Middleton sat at the bedside of his fellow lawman Renny McClaine, who had spent many weeks convalescing at Buffalo General Hospital. It was not an easy recovery, as his right hand was missing four fingers and the entire right side of his face was still bandaged; both having been torn off during a grueling battle with the feral canines under the control of the Jack Dog. The West Side Wolfman, as Mike Nero was being referred to by the press and local citizens, was involved in that bloodbath up to his furry muzzle, and Lamar had taken notice.

Renny had been conscious for some time now, but was still suffering severe bouts of pain, as evidenced by the morphine he could inject intravenously via the push of a button. He now had to do this with his left hand despite being right-handed for obvious reasons.

"The Captain doesn't want to tell me," Renny said to his friend, "but the only place for me in the force once I get out of here will be a desk job. I'm going to have to get some type of fucking prosthesis or some shit for my right hand so I can maybe still use a typewriter, or at least pick up a phone. Still, it's gonna take a good amount of physical therapy before I can do that. I may have to get some skin grafting for my face, and I may never be able to see out of my right eye again. That fucking sucks, man."

Lamar had no idea what to say to console his friend, whom he earned his badge with while going through the academy. But he was determined to keep trying because he *had* to try. He felt that he owed Renny at least that much. Part of the reason was the guilt he experienced at getting through that conflict with the Jack Dog's pack relatively intact when Renny did not, despite the latter acting no less heroically.

Lamar knew there was a word for that type of guilt in the psychology texts, but he could not recall exactly what, and he did not truly care at the moment anyway.

"Listen to me, mister," Lamar said gently but firmly. "The important thing is you proved yourself a hero no matter how short your tenure as a patrolman. Being on the streets with a gun isn't the only thing an agent of the law can do. There will always be a place for you on the force, and you're guaranteed a job with us once you get out of here. It may not be the job you signed up for, but…"

"Look, I know you mean well, Lamar. Really, I do, guy. But… you know I'm not a paper pusher or glorified secretary by nature. You've known me since high school, so you know I've always wanted an active role on the streets. This is bullshit! I can't believe this shit happened to me less than two years on the job."

"You knew the risks from the start, and you took them without hesitation. You gave a lot of yourself so that more innocent civilians didn't die. A lot of fellow cops, including my friend and my original partner, Ajay, gave their lives taking on the Jack Dog's pack. As bad as this is, you're more fortunate than they are."

Renny turned his partly covered face away. "Am I, dude? Are you sure about that?"

Lamar sighed. "Don't go there, Renny. Don't you dare."

"Why the fuck not, man? The people we lost died like warriors instead of ending up alive but missing pieces of themselves as a constant reminder they're now useless to the force! What woman is ever going to go for a failed cop who looks like he fell face first into a fucking meat grinder?"

"Renny, stop it! Once a warrior, always a warrior! You need to call on the same courage for this that you did on the field! You are not useless, you are not a failure, and there are plenty of good women who will look past those injuries to the man who sacrificed himself for every person in this city. Your courage isn't one of the parts of yourself that you lost! Right now, we need you, in one way or another. Because there is still a dangerous threat out there, one that may be part human…"

The tense conversation was interrupted when Officer Ted Bentley, Lamar's new partner since the loss of Ajay against the Jack Pack, abruptly burst into the room. And he had some important news that he knew his comrade-in-arms would be very interested in.

"Lamar, I hate to rudely end this conversation, but there's been a wolfman sighting just a few miles from here in the Lovejoy district! Do you want to check it out?"

"Does a bear want to shit in the woods? Damn straight I do!" the officer responded as he ran towards the door leading out of his fallen friend's room. "Renny, hang in there, man. I'll be back to see you soon."

"Yeah, okay," Renny softly replied. "Go and get 'im, guys."

And it really sucks a tremendously huge dick that I can't be going out there with you… now, or ever again. I need to make a seriously important decision soon. I'll… sleep on it.

So, there I was sitting on a hill in a secluded section of Walden Avenue, looking up at the waxing, nearly full moon above me. I had my "fill" for the night thanks to a certain ring-tailed animal, and now that my hunter's craving was sated, most of my human psyche was in the driver's seat.

I couldn't believe that I had actually eaten a raccoon, and I was even more startled that it didn't gross me out as much as I felt it should. I hoped I wouldn't barf or get stomach pains or something like that once I reverted to human form. Because of this fear, I decided to chill on a snow-covered hill and bask in the power of the glowing moon for a while. That would give my lupine tummy time to fully digest the animal supper I had, so there would hopefully be little of it left in my system after I turned human again.

I didn't mind staying in this powerful form as long as I could anyway, so long as I was in a secluded enough place. I also had to admit I enjoyed scaring the dookee out of people at times; to be a presence that struck fear in the hearts of others rather than usually being the intimidated one myself. And luckily, I didn't have to chill in a literal sense, since my thick, natural silvery-gray coat protected me from the bitter cold better than my heaviest winter jacket.

One thing I enjoyed about the cold season since becoming a lycanthrope was watching it snow. The falling snowflakes took on a glimmery sheen to my lupine vision, and I could make out the diverse shape of every descending flake in a manner that no ordinary human could. I had the capacity to appreciate the wonders of nature in a way that was closed to me in human form, and I found it every bit as exhilarating in its own way as the hunt.

I sat on my haunches and sniffed the chilly night air, trying to detect the scent of any nighttime straggler who might walk by and see me. If anyone did, I hoped they would simply mistake me for a big stray dog; but maybe not, since reports of a wolfman were all over the city. I just had to be wary of my surroundings, something my wolfen senses made rather easy.

As my yellowish wolfen eyes glared at the starry sky and the tumbling flakes illumined by the moonlight, I found myself wishing I had planned a new target for my mission of retribution so the activity could speed my metabolism. I wanted to digest that raccoon as fast as I could, as the fear that it might strongly disagree with my stomach upon reversion continued to pervade the human side of my thoughts. In just a moment I was to receive a lesson in the old adage to watch what you wish for.

My pointed lupine ears perked up as they detected the very subtle sound of a car tire running over a tiny pebble of gravel in the road just down the hill. To my level of hearing, it was the equivalent of what a glass bottle being smashed a few inches away would sound to a normal human.

Shit!

I turned to see exactly what I feared I would: a lone police car was quietly sneaking up behind me. I could clearly hear the muffled sound of the two occupants' voices from behind the closed windows.

"Lamar, look up the hill there!" one of them said in a low voice. "I think that's the wolfman! I only saw him once at the scene of the Jack Dog massacre, but I think that's him – or is that 'it,' man?"

Lamar? Lamar... Middleton? That's one of the cops I dealt with during that fucked up night the Jack Dog almost turned me into Gravy Train! And he's the one who said in those news interviews that he wants my furry hide! Double shit!

"Yeah, it's him!" I heard what I recognized as Lamar's voice reply. "Let's go get that mother fucker!"

Before I could react, the car doors opened and out came Lamar and his partner with firearms drawn. The gunfire sounded like mini-explosions to my ultra-sensitive ears as they pulled the triggers. I leapt off the hill on the opposite side of my assailants as the hot lead sizzled past me.

When I completed the twenty-foot drop on my two hind legs, I felt a tense pain in my left thigh that for a second made me think that maybe I tore a ligament. That was a fairly big drop, but it should have been no big deal to me in lupine form. That's when I realized I had taken a bullet, which embedded itself in the hairy flesh of my left leg.

I released a yelp of pain and fear, as I had no idea how much a regular lead bullet would hinder me or how much time it would take to heal. I also had no clue as to how I would get the damn slug out of my leg, which I figured I had to do before I reverted back to human.

"I think I hit it!" I heard Lamar's partner yell.

"It?" That fucking fuzz!

Before I could get over the mild shock and flee the scene, Lamar and his partner ran around the hill and were just a few feet to my left. And as expected, their firearms were pointed right in my direction. This time they were confronting me up close while I stood in a bipedal stance. Luckily, my nearly seven-foot bestial form clearly terrified even these brave men into immobility for a split second. I growled at them, further chilling their bones more than the wintery Buffalo air possibly could.

"Lamar, here he is! It's the fucking wolfman!"

"No shit, Ted! Open fire!"

With that order given the pain and rage finally caused my animal side to partially take over. I rushed at Lamar and the cop whose name I now knew was Ted with a swift burst of speed. It wasn't as fast as normal, considering the still-not-completely-healed bullet wound in my leg. As a result, I caught another bullet from Lamar, this one in my left shoulder, as I slammed into him like a furry freight train. The impact sent him sprawling back into his partner and both men went down hard onto the snow-covered street.

I growled angrily as I readied myself to pounce on them and use my razor-sharp talons and teeth to rip them to pieces. For some reason, however, my human side forced the animal aspect of my psyche to pause. It just seemed… wrong to slaughter two police officers who were simply doing their jobs. But they were hunting me! And they shot me twice! I couldn't just let that go!

As my animal and human side fought to make a decision, Lamar had recovered his senses and was reaching for his dropped gun. The stinging pain in my leg and shoulder convinced me I had better not let him give me a third bullet. Enough was enough!

With a swift swipe of my hand, I ripped four deep gashes in Lamar's upper arm just as his fingers closed on his piece. He shouted in agony and left the gun lying where it was to put his hand over the profusely bleeding wounds.

"Lamar, what's happenin'…?" Ted asked as he partly came out of his daze.

I leapt over Lamar and landed on my hands and lupine feet directly above the still fallen Ted, my extended wolfen muzzle just a few inches from his own face.

"I'm what's happening… you asshole!" I forced myself to mutter in a scratchy but discernible voice.

"Ahhhh shit!" Ted screamed as he braced himself for the impending agony of his face being bitten off.

And I wanted to do it. But… I didn't. As I saw the injured and bleeding Lamar scramble to retrieve his gun with his good arm, I knew it was do or die for me in the next few seconds. Or, more specifically in this case… kill or not.

I snarled in Ted's face again to terrify the fucking hell out of him and then leapt off. The adrenaline pouring through my system enabled me to ignore the discomfort of the bullet wounds and dash around the hill just as Lamar recovered his firearm.

My ears twitched at the sound of two shots fired by the cop. However, the spiking pain he was in and the obstruction of his vision from the blowing snowfall caused him to miss. I heard the lead slugs ping off the metallic hull of a streetlight a few feet behind me as I sped off down Walden Avenue to disappear into the haze of the whirling snow.

"Walter, where are you going? Isn't 8:30 rather late to be going out?"

You have always hated it when your father called you by your full name like that, Walter Lavelle. Since your childhood, it had always been a sure indicator that he was in one of *those* moods. It was the type of mindset where his lack of understanding of his son's character was going to be evident in whatever his next words happened to be.

"I'm going out to the museum, Dad," was your curt reply. "It's closed now, and all the staff is out except Chad the security guard. He said it's okay if I come down there and do some late night studies for my internship."

"But at this hour? Why can't you do the extra work during the daytime, before or between the lecture tours?"

"Because, Dad, then I have my regular studies to worry about. You know, those other scholastic subjects you have a fit if I'm not earning straight 'A's' with?"

"Watch your tone with me, young man. You know I want what's best for you…"

"Even when you have no idea what that is, right, Dad?"

Your father runs over to you as you pick your coat up off the hat rack situated by the front door. You notice he leans his arm on the top of the stand to position it in front of you as a barrier.

"What's best for everyone your age is a good education. And that means doing well in school!"

"And here I always thought it was about following your passions, whatever is most likely to get you ahead on your own terms. Isn't that what Mom always told me? You know, before she left you because of the way you are?"

You bristle with anger when your father shoves you away from the coat rack. However, he goes no further than that this time, as he has felt too many regrets for acting out in the past. This, along with the fact that you understood how he genuinely cares for you in his own way, is what prevents you from raising your hand back to him. Of course, the fact that he could thoroughly kick your ass if you did may very well be another factor which gives you pause.

I need to acquire power in this world! I am just so sick of almost everyone else in my life wielding it over me! And somehow, I just know the means of getting it is in that exhibit. I need to go there, and Dad is not *going to stop me.*

"So, what are you going to do to stop me from stepping out, Dad? Beat me? Like you did before? Like that time you lost it and slapped Mom? You know, the thing you did that finally convinced her to leave you?"

You shudder as you see your father, Bradley Lavelle, clench the fist that was not leaning on the coat rack. His eyes are filled with the type of rage that has always both terrified you and made you long to replicate its daunting fury for use on others. Rather than backing down, however, this time something deep within incites you to stand your ground. After all, is that not what one of the pharaohs like King Nebka would have done if anyone had challenged them?

After a few tension-ridden seconds of this stand-off, your dad relents. You breathe an inner sigh of relief as he unclenches his fist, and his expression softens. He then retracts his arm from the rack so that it was no longer barring your way out. It appears to you that the laments of his past actions and his unwillingness to drive away a son who would soon be eighteen causes him to enforce full self-control. For even Bradley Lavelle cannot not help but understand on some level that his past displays of temper had already driven his wife – your mother – away.

Ultimately, your father decides not to risk unleashing that inner beast of his again. Little did he know, however, that he had already long encouraged you to create a similar beast inside of yourself, Walter. It is one that has been simply waiting to acquire the power that will make you feel safe to unleash it on an unsuspecting world.

"Fine, kid," your father finally says to break the tension. "Go do what you gotta do and see if I care anymore!"

"Thank you for letting me see to that education you always say is so important, Dad," was your sarcastic reply. "Now, I have to go before I miss the bus, okay?"

You grab your coat and huff out the door before even putting it on. The biting sting of the evening's winter air causes you to quickly throw on your jacket and zipper it up. Before putting on your gloves, you briefly check the pockets of your jeans to ensure you have enough bus tokens to get you to and from the museum. Thankfully, you do, with a few to spare.

You muse to yourself that those social studies homework essays and book reports you composed for some of the popular students in school – who would have nothing of a positive nature to do with you otherwise – had paid off in some measure. As did that recent birthday gift of a new Courier CT manual portable typewriter, so those ghost assignments could be completed quickly without appearing in the wrong handwriting.

Thanks for that CT, Uncle Maurice! There are times I wish you *were my father, if only you weren't sometimes as much of a stuffy jerk as Dad is. Like him, you always talk about how you want the best for me without having the slightest understanding of what I'm actually about.*

You replace those thoughts with others as you stride purposefully to the bus stop, Walter Lavelle. These new thoughts are focused on the King Nebka exhibit, and the treasure you somehow *know* you will find hidden within the collection.

Little did you, nor the city of Buffalo, know what you would be in for after you made this fateful excursion.

You, Walter Lavelle, sat up past midnight in the museum examining the scrolls and artifacts of the new King Nebka exhibit just as you promised yourself you would. The guard on duty was generous enough to allow you to do so on his watch, even though it was technically against the rules.

You knew there must be something among the three boxes of recovered items that would allow you to access some of Nebka's power. You could just *sense* it, as if Anubis himself was guiding your eyes. You repeatedly turned to look at his nearly eight-foot mummified form as it stands unmoving in the sarcophagus that had been its prison for thousands of years. You kept the lavishly designed stone casket open, so the sight of the withered but well-preserved body was a constant reminder of the ancient majesty and power you were in the presence of.

It's certain that Nebka wasn't so abnormally tall when he was alive, you thought to yourself. *That's a common side effect of a body being in a mummified state for so long. The muscles and bones undergo some "stretching" effect I can't really explain from a physiological angle. I just know that it happens.*

Your mind then turns to other musings.

"Is your soul really trapped in there, great Nebka?" you whisper aloud to him from your desk five feet away. "Are you dead, yet still in there? I know I can read esoteric hieroglyphics enough to determine that is likely the case. I taught myself how to decipher Egyptian scripts over the years; ever since I was a kid, in fact! I don't care what that idiot archeology professor said! There's a hell of a lot of information about your civilization that establishment archeology ignores or overlooks."

You tremble as you look around to see if Chad, the guard on the midnight shift, had heard you and was on his way to investigate. After a minute, it becomes clear that he was doing rounds in another wing and thus did not hear your ranting.

Get a grip there, Walt! If Nebka really is in there, I am betting I can… make him animate again. To control him! And if the scrolls I have read really hold true, the undead state he's in will make him immensely strong. His nerve endings and remaining organs are atrophied and technically dead, so he can't actually feel physical pain, and likely no real sensations of any kind.

However, his dry, bandaged form would be very vulnerable to fire or other highly dehydrating agents, like corrosive acids; and those layers of thick wrappings need to stay on to keep his body properly preserved. But otherwise…

You take a few minutes to inspect the canopic jars. You know these small stone containers are where those who performed the mummification process placed his softer organs following their removal from the body. This would prevent them from rotting inside the corpse and disrupting the tethering of his etheric body to the remains of his physical form. They were not truly important, however. No, it was the boxes of items and scrolls your gifted but troubled mind now studies with the most intensity.

And what you would find in there would be a game-changer of immense proportions for you… as well as the entrapped consciousness of Pharaoh Nebka.

As you investigated, your eyes fell upon a curious-looking silvery amulet with a bronze chain. It had a scarlet gemstone embedded in the center. The necklace had symbols etched around the length of its circumference that you recognize as the *'was'* sceptre, one of the symbols of Anubis.

The jackal-headed deity's governance over Egyptian funerary rites and embalming processes, as well as his control over the soul's passage into the Duat, *would have been invoked by powerful high priests to entrap the etheric body of a spirit in its preserved material body. And I swear I can* feel *such necromantic energies infused into that amulet!*

Then the realization hits you like a thrown boulder. "My gods, can it be? Can it really be one of *those* necklaces?"

You excitedly rifle through the pages of one of your own books, eager to compare what you have just found with what you recall having read in a tome that you own.

It was a godsend when I managed to find this ancient tome at that strange curio shop a few months ago. That's where I learned of the necklaces! According to the text, there were a small number of them created by some of the most skilled high priests throughout the dynasties of ancient Egypt. They utilized the power of Anubis to enhance the psychic abilities of its wearer. The amulet would enable them to "connect" on an etheric level with the consciousness trapped in one of these "cursed" mummies.

Depending on the necklace's specific design, the wearer could either re-animate and control the mummy through the force of their own will; or they could actually project their consciousness out of their body and into the mummy, animating it and using its powerful form as if it were their own. Their physical body would go into a trance that "froze" its metabolism so that it would not require food or water etc., as long as the wearer's mind remained within the intact mummy. They could then project their psyche back into their own body, returning the mummy to it immobile state.

I remember reading reports of such a necklace being found and used a few times by different people in the past. One was in Egypt near the turn of the century, while a few years later another guy found his consciousness trapped in a mummy's body during a rampage in Boston. Another such incident occurred as recently as the past decade, after that necklace was found by some woman in a Boston museum. I have no idea if these reports are true, but… I think they are! Oh, my gods, could this be such a necklace?

It looks like the one in the book illustration here. Also, a bit different though, because of that red-colored gem.

The symbol that the jewel has embroidered in its center is an ankh staff alongside an upraised mummified hand inscribed with green coloring. These are symbols of Ptah, the ultimate creator-deity of the Egyptian pantheon; in fact, he is believed by some scholars to be nothing less than a personification of the universal creator-force itself that was later granted additional attributes, such as the lord of craftsmen.

Directly underneath Ptah's symbols is what looks like a jackal's head but inscribed in white paint. That suggests it's symbolizing the god Wepwawet, "the opener of the ways," sometimes considered the son of Anubis and having power over travel. The fact that his symbol is directly underneath those of Ptah implies to me that whichever mystic of the priesthood crafted this necklace believed Wepwawet to also be connected with the creator-god, possibly an avatar thereof. So, he's apparently shown to be drawing on the power of Ptah to increase his own mastery over gateways and travel.

"But this jewel!" you say to yourself aloud. "There are some inscriptions on the necklace that, when translated in the scroll here, says that it's a portion of the same meteorite that the fabled bauble called the Jewel of Seven Stars was made from. That's the one which had become the property of none other than Queen Tera during the 11th Dynasty."

Queen Tera! She was nothing less than amazing! Surviving information on her first uncovered by this Dutch explorer called Van Huyn when he traveled to Egypt during the 17th Century revealed that she was not only one of the few women to rule ancient Egypt as a pharaoh but had great magickal power.

Much of that power was courtesy of the Jewel of Seven Stars, which this gem is a fragment of. Rumor has it she still walks the Earth today thanks to being given a mystical "awakening" in 1903 by some scholar and mystic wannabe named Abel Trelawny – but as incredible as that possibility is, it's still not my main concern here! That concern would be having a portion of that jewel itself, no matter how small, to enhance the forces of this amulet!

It was then, after a few minutes of having picked up and closely examined the necklace, that you sense what appeared to be a "pull" from the object. The sensation seems to be occurring on the psychic level, as if an inaudible but still somewhat discernible voice were begging you to put the necklace on. You look to Nebka's mummy as if his entrapped soul is the source of the "voice," its communication with you made possible via the Amulet of Anubis. You have no need for such persuasion, however, as you already had every intention of donning it and testing its validity for yourself.

Now that the amulet is around your neck, the echoey voice suddenly becomes strangely audible, yet still occurring in your "head" rather than reaching your ears through physically projected sound waves.

"Now… focus!" the voice seems to command in thought waves that can transcend any language barrier.

You turn to the mummy, which you now know is most definitely the source. This provides you with all the confirmation you need that the consciousness of Nebka is indeed trapped within the preserved cadaver. However, it seems to be in a state of semi-slumber, for want of a better description. As you further focus your concentration, you can actually perceive a mental image of a fearsome but handsome face appear in your brain. It has dark skin and equally dark eyes that are absolutely penetrating. The image is wearing a *nemes* – the distinctive striped headdress of a pharaoh.

"Nebka."

"Focus… project… join me in this body. Let us be… one. Let my power… be our power!"

"Yes! It's true!" you said aloud as you shut your eyes tightly and began focusing as directed.

As you did so, more than one strange sensation occurred. On one level, you felt your consciousness disconnect from your unimpressive living body and felt as if it were rapidly floating towards a new destination. You knew this was a result of the power of Anubis.

At the same time, you can detect an intense vibration about you, as if you were being disassembled on a molecular level. By way of the same form of psychic understanding as before, you know this to be the power of Wepwawet, drawing further universal energy from Ptah.

It is transporting your physical body from one place to another with a speed that is close to instantaneous. Those of lesser understanding might have another word for it: teleportation – or, considering what you would soon discover had actually occurred – quantum "exchange."

When you open your eyes, you still appear to be sitting on the same chair as before. Yet you feel distinctly different. Somehow you seem to be much bigger in size, and your limbs feel somewhat stiff but immensely powerful. You lift your hands in front of you and to your astonishment they were indeed quite large… and wrapped in bandages!

Before you could fully grasp the situation, the old wooden chair collapses under your now far greater weight. You land hard on the floor, yet you feel no pain, or even any jolt from the impact. You stand up with a bit of difficulty, your movements gradually adjusting to and eliminating the stiffness in these much larger and stronger limbs. You repeatedly clamp and unclench your fingers on each hand to expedite this process.

You quickly come to understand that you are indeed considerably taller than before. As you turn to look at the sarcophagus, what you see inside the ancient stone casket shocks you to the core of your being, more so than anything that has happened since you found the necklace.

Standing in the golden casket in place of Nebka's mummy, but in an identical position with crossed arms, was your body. That is, the thin, unathletic, and far shorter form of Walter Lavelle, the body you called your own until mere seconds ago. Around your true body's neck was the amulet. The eyes were closed, and your human form looked to be in a deep torpor.

You open your mouth to utter an exclamation, but the atrophied larynx in the body you now possess produces no sound. Hence, you "hear" your intended words only in the form of thoughts.

Oh, my gods! My mind is in the body of the mummy! And my human form literally traded places with it! I mean, my real body is now in the sarcophagus! That must have been what the Gem of Ptah, chiseled from the Jewel of Seven Stars, added to this amulet!

It had to be the source of the strange "moving" sensation I felt, as if I was being deconstructed or pulled through some type of invisible gate. It exchanged me and the mummy physically in time and space, with such speed that it seemed almost instantaneous.

What would happen next, Walter Lavelle, would be your first true step on the path to darkness.

You suddenly find yourself roundly startled as the security guard you know only as Chad opens the door to the exhibit room.

"What the hell happened in here, Walt?"

It is then that the man finds himself staring not at your body, but beholding the towering, horrifying form of the mummy your consciousness now controls. Chad's jaw drops as he stares in dumbfounded terror at the monstrosity that stands before him. And that monstrosity is *you*, Walter Lavelle!

Oh shit! Chad must've heard the chair break and come to investigate!

That is when the still present psyche of Nebka first begins urging you to "do something" about the situation, lest the plans you both harbor be cast in ruin. And what he urges you to do first is nothing less than murder.

"Extinguish… intruder!"

Aw, man, I can't do that! He didn't mean any harm…

"Do it!"

"Oh god! The mummy… walks!" Chad exclaims in panic. "How can it be walking? It's not possible!"

The guard, who was certified to carry a firearm, reaches for the weapon in his holster. It is now your turn to panic, Walter.

Chad, no! Don't! But no sound issues forth from your dried, desiccated throat.

The terror-stricken guard pulls the trigger and fires two shots of hot lead into your bandaged upper torso. You back away an inch or two from the impact, but though the leaden projectiles have pierced the tight wrappings around your chest and the shriveled flesh underneath, you feel no pain and no blood oozes from the wounds.

This, you realize, is because the dead body you now inhabit is bereft of nerve endings and flowing blood; hence, you suffer but the barest hint of discomfort and no crippling damage. The attack has still rattled and enraged you, however. And the mind of King Nebka, having learned of what firearms are from your memories that are now conjoined with his own, further fuels your anger.

I told you not to do that, Chad!

Only you and the semi-cognizant mind of Nebka "hear" those words of yours, Walter. Nevertheless, Chad still experiences your ire, albeit on a much more physical level.

The form you now inhabit moves towards the security guard with surprising speed for such a large frame. You bring your fist down atop the much shorter man's head. His skull crumples under your blow as if it had been struck by a pile driver. The man you knew only as Chad slumps to the floor with blood spilling out every orifice and staining the beige tiled surface of the floor.

His cranium is so severely bashed inwards that his gray matter becomes clearly visible to you through the ghastly wound that *you* inflicted upon his fragile human skull.

If you had an operative gastric system in this form, Walter, you likely would have vomited upon the floor upon seeing this ghastly handiwork of yours. Instead, you can only express the horror over what you have done with an expression on the mummy's hideous wrinkled face. That look only lasts a few seconds, however. You have now committed your first murder, Walter. And having done so while in the proverbial driver's seat of the mummy's unliving but incredibly strong body makes you feel *powerful*.

You have finally gotten a taste of the power you have craved for so long, Walter. You have the whims of the gods and the motivating psyche of the ruthless King Nebka to thank for this. You see that there is so much you could accomplish with this power, and so much you *would* accomplish.

I gotta get back to my own body and get the hell out of here before what's left of Chad is discovered in the morning. With the power in this amulet, I can make the exchange anywhere I happen to be. I know that! I'm in charge of inventory in this exhibit, so I'll just make no record of this necklace being among the items.

Before reversing the exchange, you look back down at the carcass of the security guard. His shattered skull is still dribbling cranial matter onto the floor and his glazed eyes are opened wide, as if to give you a strong accusatory glare.

Sorry, Chad. But I had to do this. I hope you can understand.

You maneuver the mummy's huge body into standing still as you focus on the power of the amulet that tethered your consciousness to your entranced real body. Once again, you feel your psyche flow out of the mummy and back into your original form. At the same time, you feel yourself being strongly "pulled," which you know is the closest word you can think of to describe the sensation of your original body exchanging physical space with the mummy.

In what seems like a mere moment to you, your eyes open, and your mind is back in your weak but proper living body. You are not in the sarcophagus but standing where the mummy had been a moment ago. You look to the stone tomb beside you to see Nebka's grotesque bandaged form back in the casket with arms crossed over his chest. You close the baroque coffin and quietly make your way out of the museum, taking with you the necklace and your personal effects so no one would know you were there.

Only poor Chad knew of your presence after closing time, having allowed you to stay for an after-hour study session in the exhibit room against his better judgment. It was a gracious decision that cost him the heaviest price imaginable.

Now I'll show the world who has the power…

***

Lamar winced several times as Doctor Huey Eggert stitched up the four deep gashes on his upper right arm.

"I'm sorry if this hurts, but those are some really bad gashes there, Officer Middleton," the doctor stated.

"I don't mean to come off like a baby, Doc, but getting your bicep ripped open by a werewolf is no joke."

"No doubt it isn't, Officer. Try to keep that arm steady now, okay? If a local anesthetic would help…"

"No, I'm good here, Doctor. That goddamned thing would have to tear into my shooting arm, though. Now I'll have to compensate for that until I heal up. I swear I'm gonna kill that no good hairy bastard."

"Steady, okay?"

The doctor was clearly not concerned if this cop really had a run-in with the already legendary West Side Wolfman or not; his job was simply to patch up the wounds and let the police deal with the rest.

"Oww! Damn, Doc!"

"I said to try to keep steady, Officer."

A young, somewhat heavy set blonde nurse named Eve then walked into the room to deliver the sterile gauze wrappings that the doctor requested.

"Wow, those are some nasty ass gashes you got there," she remarked to the policeman. "How'd you get them?"

"I have a really itchy rash," Lamar spat, "and I've been scratching it too much."

Eve made a half-frown. "Hmmm."

"Okay, sorry for the sarcasm. I had a run-in with the wolfman tonight, and he ripped me a good one."

"Oh," she replied. "Did you get him too?"

"My partner and I both shot him, but I don't think he's dead. If that's what you're asking."

"Oh. Hmmm."

After that, Eve quietly departed. Almost immediately the door into the emergency room swung open again and Captain Jean Rogen stormed in.

"Middleton, what the hell is going on?" she queried. "I talked to Bentley, but he's not making much sense. His report says you two got attacked by that werewolf supposedly running around the city."

"Not just 'supposedly,' Captain," Lamar retorted with frustration. "I saw the damn thing twice now, including during the big final bash with the Jack Pack last month. So did Ted and Renny, along with the other two officers who survived, Cary and Hilbert. We all filed reports."

"Yes, I know you all did, Middleton. And I read them. But I'm not convinced that what you saw then, and had an altercation with tonight, is an actual bona fide werewolf instead of just a leftover from the Jack Dog's pack."

"Hold steady, Officer!" Dr. Eggert again complained. "I'm almost done here."

"Doctor, while your ministrations are both appreciated and necessary," Captain Rogen told the physician, "please do finish up, as I need to have a conversation with Officer Middleton, okay?"

"I won't rush, Captain," the doctor said firmly.

Rogen sighed but offered no further griping.

After another twenty seconds, the physician tied and cut the twine of the stiches, and the procedure was completed.

"I'm done, Officer," he said. "Try to rest up until you heal, and come back if there are any problems, including signs of infection. On the other hand, please do not come back if you start growing fur and sprouting fangs."

Doctor Eggert displayed a mirthful smile, which quickly turned into a frown when he saw the glares both Lamar and Rogen were giving him.

"Uh, you have the room, Captain," Eggert said as he quickly departed.

"Okay, Middleton," the captain continued. "Why are you so certain that we're dealing with an actual werewolf, rather than just another big and strangely bred feral canine, like the Jack Dog? Renny's report didn't actually include mention of a werewolf. Hilbert and Carey said they had no idea what they saw battling the Jack Dog; they guessed it could have a strong canine competitor for the alpha of the pack.

"The same with Bentley at the time. It's only now, after the incident earlier tonight, that he's agreeing with you about a werewolf. He says at one point it stood on two legs like a man and that it actually… talked?"

"Yes, Captain, it did both those things. I saw and heard exactly what Ted did."

"Weren't you freshly injured at the time, and experiencing terrible pain? And wasn't Bentley terrified out of his mind, as the animal had jumped on him when you supposedly heard this?"

"I understand what you're getting at, ma'am. But both of us heard it talk, and both of us heard it say the same thing. We couldn't have experienced something identical, even if we were both out of our minds at the time. Our reports were too consistent, don't you agree?"

The captain simply looked at him, her dark brown eyes and short brown hair with just a bit of gray at the temples highlighted under the fluorescent lights of the room. Lamar and most of the force serving under her always found that look, and her appearance in general, to be unsettlingly intimidating. She was a tough, no-nonsense cop who truly earned her reputation and rank after years of service in the BPD.

"How bad is your injury? What did Dr. Eggert say?"

"You mean, besides the endless variations of 'keep that arm steady, please' as he sewed me up? He said it was bad enough, but not life-threatening, and not career-ending. He can't be certain right now if there may be some nerve damage – permanent or otherwise – so, we'll just have to wait and see, I guess."

Suddenly, he knew *exactly* how Renny felt. It made his stomach boil over.

"You and Bentley both said you shot it?"

"Yeah, we did. Twice, as in, one time each. And the bullets didn't stop it. I told you in my report last month we should request shipments of silver bullets from the state government. We need to arm all Buffalo precincts, and maybe even those in the surrounding 'burbs, with silver ammo. And maybe even billy clubs with silver knobs on the end."

Rogen sighed again. "Middleton – Lamar… let's be practical here. Do you know how much a large shipment of bullets made of genuine silver would cost? Let alone those other silver implements you suggested? Also, are you aware that silver is not as efficient as lead when it comes to providing ammo for a firearm?"

"Modifications have to be made then, Captain."

"Which runs into more money!"

"That shouldn't be an object when it comes to the safety of both your officers and the people of the city we have taken an oath to protect… ma'am."

"Well, money *is* an important thing in the world we live in and protect, Officer Middleton! Like it or not, right or wrong, that is the reality. Convincing the state government that there is a real supernatural werewolf running loose that would justify such an expenditure when cuts are already being made across the board would be the tallest of orders! That is quite a position you're putting the administration in, mister!"

Lamar bit his tongue *hard* and thought carefully before responding. He made a point to remind himself of exactly who he was speaking to here; not only her rank, but the person behind it.

"Then… I guess we'll have to make do without your help, and without the help of the state of New York. Ma'am."

With that, the embittered officer stood up and began walking out of the room.

"I need the doctor's report to see if you're fit for duty health-wise, Middleton! Keep that in mind."

Unfortunately, he was out the door without bothering to give a response. Rogen gritted her teeth, but in consideration for all he went through on behalf of the city earlier, she decided to let his attitude go. This time, at least.

I growled in pain as I sat in a backyard on Bailey Avenue while jabbing the talons of my left index finger and thumb into my shoulder wound. It was a desperate bid to rip into myself and remove the bullets – starting with my shoulder – before reverting to human. It was, as I suspected, difficult and quite painful, as the gaping holes made by the lead bullets had mostly healed over around the slugs before I found a darkened backyard that was not illuminated by a deck bulb or Christmas lights.

So, in effect, I had to mostly re-open the wound, or likely create a new one from scratch.

I hoped this damn supernatural healing ability of mine had at least partially expelled the bullets, so that they were conveniently a lot less deep in the flesh now than they were at first. I realized that I needed to grind my teeth and resist the pain to get this done as quickly as I could. I couldn't wait for my enhanced system to expel the bullets entirely, especially when the muscle tissue kept healing around them.

As I hoped, the bullet in my shoulder was closer to the surface of the outer furry dermis than when I first got shot. My finger and thumb finally felt it, and I did my best to stay silent as I dug down just a bit further. Finally, my steely digits got a good enough grip on the slug and I tore it out with a sudden pull.

"Graarrrrr!" Okay, that hurt. Shit. Shit mother fucker.

I tossed the blood-covered and deformed projectile away. The wound would quickly heal again. That wasn't a concern of mine at the present, however. My new concern was going through the routine a second time with the bullet in my thigh.

Please let it be further to the surface of the flesh now! Fenris, give me strength to do this.

"Grrrrr…!" *Geez, Nero, you're a frickin' fearsome werewolf, for gods' sake, not a little baby! Man up! Or wolf up! Whatever.*

It seemed I had to dig my sharpened index and thumb nails even further into the flesh of my thigh than my shoulder to get that damn bullet.

Shit, the wound had completely healed over. I gotta tear into myself and create a new one. This is not gonna be pleasant…

"Grrarrrrr!" I was a master of understatement, as always.

The slug was finally out, though. I tossed the small but deadly piece of metal into a pile of snow. I then laid down on the snowy grass, waiting for my leg wound to fully heal again. My shoulder injury was almost completely repaired once more, so that was good, at least.

I really need to plan for contingencies like this. And I really need to be thankful that those bullets weren't silver.

My lupine ears then perked up as I heard the back door of the house thrown open. Just my luck the two young men who rushed out were wearing what I recognized as the distinctive bandanas and jackets of the dangerous street gang known as the Red Dragons. To make matters worse, one was carrying a shotgun, and the other what I think was a .45 pistol.

I should have considered the area I was in, dammit!

"I know I heard something out here!" the first one, a muscular black man, said. "Sounded like a dog having a fucking orgasm, or something!"

Errr, that asshole! I had to force myself not to growl again, this time in anger. I knew that I needed to try and get out of this without tangling with these guys.

"You think it's one of those stray feral dogs?" the second one, a tall, thin but athletic-looking white guy asked. "I thought the pigs went and killed them all a month ago?"

"Maybe. Maybe not," the first one replied. "Maybe it's that dang werewolf."

The tall white gangbanger started laughing. "Seriously, bro? That wolfman shit ain't real. It was just a really *ugly* member of that dog pack. Think it could be one of our competition?"

"You mean the State Boys? They better stay the fuck out of our turf. We warned them! But as much as I'd like to blow a hole in one of those mother fuckers tonight, they're still people, and people don't make animal sounds like that."

My leg felt closer to being healed. I needed to make a run on all fours and leap over that fence before they could start shooting. It was already past 11 PM, and I knew that my mother and my stepdad were gonna shit bricks as it is when I walked in so late. And it was going to take me over twenty minutes to run home from here even if I could go at my top speed.

My course of action decided, I leapt atop the large snowbank to use it as a springboard to propel myself over the large wooden fence dividing this yard from the neighbor's. Unfortunately, it was just my luck (again) that the mound of snow couldn't hold my weight and it collapsed underneath me. I landed on the grass with a loud thud and a cloud of scattered snow. That display of sound and white mist alerted both of the gang members, who were standing only fifteen feet away.

"Shit, man!" the taller one hollered. "It *is* the fucking werewolf! Look, man!"

"Sweet Christmas!" the burly one exclaimed as he saw the same thing his partner did. "We gotta kill it!"

No! I am not *going to let them shoot me! I'm not gonna get shot again tonight!*

The wolfen side of my psyche took over and I howled in rage as I dashed at them on all fours. The taller one managed to get off a shot with his .45, but his state of mind caused him to miss. I made sure to run towards them in a zig-zagging motion to make that more likely to occur. I then leapt through the air and landed on him, my hefty weight taking him down instantly. My enhanced auditory capacity clearly heard at least two of his ribs splintering like decayed twigs.

I jumped off him as he screamed and coughed up a wad of blood. It's possible that one of his lungs was punctured.

At least it caused him to drop his piece, but that still left the more muscular guy with the shotgun as a threat. He was reluctant to blast me while I was on top of his friend since he knew the spray of buckshot would perforate his fellow gang member along with me. But I knew I couldn't count on that level of consideration to last.

"You fucker!" the big-muscled man yelled as he pointed the long barrel of the shotgun at me and pulled the trigger.

I jumped off his friend just in time to avoid taking the brunt of the spray, but some of the buckshot still struck my right leg. Again, this happened! I howled in pain-wracked fury as I landed a dozen feet away on another snowbank.

"Shit, Marty, I'm sorry, man!" the gangbanger shouted as he saw how he had riddled his friend's arm, hip, and side with pellets.

The guy identified as Marty screamed and writhed in pain while the snow on his right side became stained with crimson. The pain of myself getting shot – again! – threw me into such a state of anger that the animal side completely took over.

I ran at the more muscular gang member faster than he could get a grip and target me with his shotgun again. I slammed into him, easily knocking the obviously strong man over. He dropped his weapon and grasped my muzzle with both hands and held it firmly. A surge of adrenalin gave his impressive musculature a surprising amount of strength as he desperately tried to keep my teeth from sinking into him.

It was a valiant effort from a warrior of the streets that ultimately didn't pan out. My human-like hands were still free and slashed him with my talons several times across his upper chest, face, and neck. He shrieked in agony as his flesh was torn from him in at least a half dozen places. Several mini-fountains of blood gushed from each of the wounds, and it stained my grayish coat, the snow surrounding us, and his own clothing a bright crimson. I then wrenched my muzzle out of his grip and bit down on his wrist, crushing the radius and trapezoid into mere fragments of bone.

I jumped off the gravely injured dude and fled the yard before the sounds of the gunfire and their screams attracted more members of the gang who may also have been residing in that house. Though my right leg suffered a stinging pain from the myriad of small pellets embedded in the flesh, the adrenaline flowing through my veins gave me sufficient resistance to depart the area comprising the Red Dragons' turf entirely.

Damn, how the hell am I going to get all that buckshot out of me before reverting to human?

You arrived at the museum the next morning knowing what you would see, Walter Lavelle: a crime scene as police and forensic scientists investigated Chad's murder. A murder *you* were responsible for. However, you had to keep up the pretense of ignorance and not engage in any suspicious behavior. No one knew you had been there, save for the man who is now too dead to tell anyone. You could actually hear the psychic laugher of Nebka, whose consciousness was still connected to yours on a subliminal level, for your following his lead in showing one of the peasants of the present era who was the master, the *king*.

You had a few mixed emotions regarding the dictates of the pharaoh you admired while you walked into the building, but they were soon cast aside in favor of more pragmatic concerns. You did understand that you would be asked questions, and you did your best to look shocked and even saddened at the "news" of Chad's brutal murder.

"But who could have done this, Captain?" you asked Jean Rogen through weepy crocodile tears as she spoke to you.

"Let me ask the questions, young man," she told you brusquely. "You've been doing an internship here, right?"

"I have, yes." You then feigned wiping tears from your eyes.

"How well did you know Mr. Wilson?"

"You mean, Chad?" You did your best to look as if you knew him as little as possible, as you were actually well aware of his surname. "I only knew him vaguely. I wasn't ever really on talking terms with him. He seemed like a nice man, though, so I can't believe…"

"Was everyone else you knew here a nice person?"

"Huh?"

"I meant, did you know anyone who displayed suspicious or strange behavior, or may have had a grudge against Mr. Wilson?"

"No, no. Everyone seemed so nice. Did… did someone try to rob the place, maybe? And Chad surprised them? Could that be what happened?"

"If someone did, it was an inside job. No alarms were set off, and there is no sign of forced entry. So, back to the questions. Where were you last night?"

"I was in bed sleeping."

"Do you live with your parents?"

"Just my dad."

"Any siblings or other relatives staying there with you?"

"No."

"Could your dad verify you were at home sleeping last night?"

"Oh, dear gods, Captain! Are – are you accusing me of something?" You managed to perform another convincing act of tear-shedding.

"Take it easy, kid. I have to ask these questions to everyone who is associated with this place. That includes all employees and interns. It's just procedure, don't take it personally."

"But come on now, Captain. Does this look like something I could actually do?"

Rogen could not help but feel just a bit bad at seeing a fragile-looking young man like you go to pieces due to her gruff line of questioning, Walter. She was very hard-hearted, but not entirely without compassion, as you hoped. So, she decided to answer that one question of yours.

"Actually, young man… no, it doesn't. Whoever did this to Mr. Wilson had to be big and very strong. You… don't fit that bill, to be honest."

Good, so she isn't going to call my dad and ask him if I was home or not last night!

You pushed yourself to cry again. "This… is terrible, Captain Rogen. I didn't think anything like this could happen at a nice museum like this. I'm sorry, but… I think I'm gonna be sick."

"Alright, go to one of the restrooms on the other side of the museum. Do what you gotta do there and then go home, okay? Wait to hear from the curator before you come back here again."

"Okay. Thank you, Captain."

You rushed in the direction where you knew one of the restrooms was located in a wing distant from the Nebka exhibit, the latter of which was cordoned off by police. You entered the restroom, took a few minutes to splash water on your face from the sink to make it appear you did *something* in there, and then exited the museum altogether.

I'm sorry again, Chad. You didn't leave me any choice. I'm sure Osiris will take that into consideration when he judges you in the Duat. *If that's where you end up, of course.*

Anyway, as much as I would love to look for further enchanted artifacts and special scrolls in the exhibit, it may be sometime before I can go back there. Hopefully, the investigation by the police turns up nothing that leads to me. How could it, though? And even if it does... well, I apologize ahead of time, Captain Rogen, but I can't let you and the other cops ruin my plans.

The most important thing is that I got the necklace. I'll keep it tucked in my shirt, so nobody really notices it. And the mummy can stay right where it is, in the sarcophagus, because this little amulet can do the mental and physical exchange wherever I may be.

No one should see my regular body appear in the sarcophagus as long as it doesn't get opened during a tour of the exhibition during one of my exchanges. I'll have to do my best to only make the exchange during the night, and as briefly as possible during the day if I ever need the power of the mummy then.

As you walked out of the museum, you ran into the study group of high school students who had quickly left the building due to the unexpected situation. Kendra was among them, and your heart skipped several beats the moment you saw her; you had never in your life beheld a girl more stunning. Now that you had increased confidence with the power of the mummy at your beck and call, you worked up the courage to approach her as she stood among the crowd gathered outside.

"Hey, Kendra!" you greeted her eagerly.

"Oh, hey, Walt," she replied with less enthusiasm, but still trying to sound friendly.

"I'm sorry class got canceled for such a reason, and my heart goes out to Chad's family. Still, I'm glad to see you here."

"What a thing to happen! Do you know how he died? I heard he was murdered or something. My god."

"I don't know exactly what happened, but it's a terrible loss. Anyway, I'm glad I ran into you here."

"Oh, yea?"

"Yes. I figured we have time to talk with the museum class being canceled and all."

"Okay. Talk about what?"

"Well... I really am glad to see you. And seeing you always makes me smile."

"Okay."

Stop being so awkward, man! Be confident! You have the power to protect her like no one else can. You are now worthy of her with the power you have! You possess the ability to destroy anyone who messes with her. Or anyone who messes with you. You have power now, just like King Nebka and the other pharaohs did. You are somebody *now.*

With that thought, you found your voice again. "Look, Kendra, we should go to the coffee shop down the block. It'll be my treat, and it'll be a comfy place to talk."

"Thank you for that offer, but I should be getting home. I'm a bit frazzled by what happened at the museum."

"I know, and it was an awful thing to happen. But I could help take your mind off it and talk about other things..."

Suddenly, you heard another, all-too familiar voice ring out of the crowd. "Yo, Kendra! Is Walt bothering you?"

It was none other than Vance Jacobs. And beside him, as usual, was Edwin Tanner.

Dammit! I should have known that they would be here too. Damn them!

"Um, no, Vance," Kendra answered. "He's okay. He wants to treat me at the coffee shop, and you two can come with us."

Your teeth involuntarily gnashed together when you heard her extend the invitation to them.

"Hey, cool! I like coffee," Edwin said.

"Since I was gonna ask you to hang anyways," Vance said, "we'll tag along." Then he turned to you, his good looks and pearly smile both mocking you. "And don't worry about having to spend, Walt. I'll treat her at the shop."

"I *have* the money, Vance," you replied curtly.

"Well, cool," he said. "In that case, since you have the cash and you're feeling so generous today, you can treat Edwin."

"Fuckin' a, man," Edwin responded with a grin.

"Yea, you can just treat Edwin, Walt," Kendra agreed with a smile. "Vance was probably going to end up treating me today before I ran into you. And I'll treat him next time."

"No need," Vance said with another clean pearly smile.

"Look, guys," you affirmed, no longer able to keep your patience. "My offer was for just Kendra to hang with me. I want to talk to her... alone."

"Ha ha, okay," Vance replied. "So, is that what you want, Kendra?"

"Actually, Walt, I think that's kinda rude of you," she responded. "Vance and Edwin are my friends. I was already planning on hanging with them today. I don't really know you that well, at least not compared to them. And I'd feel better if they were there. There's no reason we can't all hang out together."

"Word!" Vance exclaimed with a smirk.

Edwin walked a bit closer to you for his retort. "I think what she means, guy, is that she doesn't want to get to know you better. So, if you wanna hang with her, you hang with us too. You're creeping her out, man."

"Now, I didn't say that, Ed," Kendra stated.

"Well, not in so many words," Edwin said. "But why beat around the bush? He's a big boy, he can handle the truth. I figure I can at least give him the benefit of the doubt, right? Heh."

Those dicks! Okay, I need to stop being a wuss if I want her to respect me. They don't know it, but I now have a lot more power than they do.

"Kendra, do these guys speak for you?" was your query to her. "I believe you can think for yourself. I respect your ability to do that, even if they don't."

You noticed that Vance was now getting flustered with you. "Yeah, tell the little fag – oops, I mean, the exhibition guide who doesn't know his shit – what you really think, Kendra."

"Vance!" she exclaimed, before turning to you. "Look, Walt, I'm sorry this happened, but to keep it from getting worse, I'm going to go hang with just Vance and Edwin, like I originally planned. We have some studying to do anyway. Maybe some other time we can all hang together, okay?"

You were now beginning to visibly tremble. You could again "hear" Nebka's authoritative voice inside your own mind, spurring you on and seeking to influence you.

"Do not tolerate such beetle dung hurled at you from these foolish plebians. I had men killed for lesser affronts. You know what must be done, Walter. Do not be the man-bitch which those fools implied."

"Edwin…" you said, trying to keep your temper in check, knowing this feeble human body of yours was not the vessel required to make things right. "I'm not a fag. Okay?"

The young man simply grinned again. "Okay, man. If you say so."

"Alright," Kendra interjected, "let's just go. No more macho shit here, okay?"

The two boys began laughing as they walked away from you with Kendra in their company. You noticed how physically close she got to Vance as they did so. Your body was now trembling with rage all the more, which you fought to keep in check just a little bit longer.

Yes. I know what to do, Nebka. Thank you for giving me the confidence to do it.

Edwin sat in his backyard clubhouse playing *Pac-Man* on his Atari 2600, which was hooked up to a small hand-me-down black and white TV set. Also present was Edwin's cousin Dex and longtime friend Billy. This clubhouse had been built by him and his dad many years earlier, and it had since become a well-known hang-out spot for local teens in his circle who were looking for intimate privacy, illegal drinking, and video game fun without having to lose scores of quarters at the local arcades.

His dad, a professional linesman by vocation, had installed two working outlets connected to the main house, so the structure had electricity for a television, a lamp, and a big space heater – the latter making the clubhouse a viable place to spend time even on a cold Friday evening such as this.

Of course, being the smart and inquisitive young man you are, Walter Lavelle, you had learned of this place over the past year. It was never kept a secret from you, as it was not only too well-known among your social group, but it almost seemed as if Edwin received some pleasure out of you knowing about it but never being invited.

The neighborhood, a better one than you lived in, was lit up merrily with Christmas lights and glowing decorations. Images of Santa Claus, the benevolent seasonal deity, were all around… but he was not the god whose powers you would be invoking this night. Because of the readily available illumination, you cautiously approached the house after busing to the area.

You had earlier taken several pictures of the neighborhood with your Polaroid – all so you could study the lay of the land. That enabled you to figure out a way to surreptitiously enter Edwin's backyard on this Friday evening when you knew he would be present in the clubhouse.

You had no idea who would be partying there with him, but you hoped they would stay out of the mummy's way when you used Nebka's mighty form to do what you needed to do. The sight of this towering, bandaged abomination would give them pause, and provide you with the thrill of knowing that others feared you.

Your research paid off, as you discreetly entered his yard by carefully scaling a few small fences. It was 10:00 PM and most people in this neighborhood were retired for the evening. You were soon standing just several feet away from the clubhouse, in a position where you could not be seen outside of its sole glass-covered window.

You saw it was a well-constructed but drab looking structure that could comfortably hold up to two dozen people, and you knew from conversations you overheard that it had a door with a heavy wooden bolt lock. You pulled your winter coat around you to fend off the chill, realizing that in a few moments you would be in a new body that had no nerve endings to detect and be bothered by freezing temperatures.

After finding a spot behind a large snowbank you stood quietly, closed your eyes, crossed your arms, and focused your mind on the amulet. As before when you conducted this ritual, you felt both your consciousness float free of your body and the sensation of an intense "pulling" sensation enveloping you.

When you opened your lids again, you were seeing through the dull gray eyes of the mummy. You were much bigger and far stronger than before, and you no longer felt the stinging bite of the cold, or any other tactile sensations for that matter. Moreover, you could sense the psyche of Nebka pushing you towards your dark goal.

Several minutes earlier in the clubhouse, the three young men continue their revelry, with Billy playing *Pac-Man,* Dex was sitting beside him watching and waiting for his turn at the joystick, and Edwin lounged at the small picnic table behind them sipping a beer. They had no idea of what lurked outside, expecting this evening to be like any other.

"Geez, this game sucks!" Billy complains. "It's nothing like the arcade version! What a rip-off!"

"Chill out, dude," Edwin says in response. "You know that home systems don't have the memory to make the games exactly like the arcade version. Especially not the Atari!"

"Well, why didn't you get a better system, like Intellivision or the Odyssey2?" Dex enquires. "I heard they're better."

"Not by much," Edwin replies, "and besides, Atari has the most games. If you want to bitch about how they aren't as good as the arcade versions, then go to one of those places and waste a hundred quarters a night on the 'real' *Pac-Man.* This may be the shitty version, but at least here you can play for free."

"Hey, wasn't that hottie Kendra supposed to be here tonight, man?" Billy asks as the digital Pac-Man avatar he controlled on the screen is struck and nullified by one of the nondescript ghosts. "Shit! It always gets me there!"

"Yeah, I invited her," Edwin answers. "But she decided to go to the Vermillion Room tonight, because she knew Vance would be there. You know she's got the major hots for him. And he wanted to go there tonight instead of here, which is why she's there and not here too."

"Bummer," Dex says. "Vance always has all the luck."

"Yeah, but he shares the wealth often enough," Edwin remarks with a smirk. "So, who am I to complain?"

"You should be complaining about how much money you wasted on this piece of shit game," Billy comments. "I can't believe Atari gets away with passing this thing off as *Pac-Man!* Shit, he's not supposed to have eyes!"

"Oh, stop your bitchin', man," is Edwin's retort as he guzzles down the remainder of the beer in the can.

A split second later the heavily bolted door was smashed inwards with a single blow from the mummy. The mummy *you* controlled, Walter.

"Holy Geez!" Billy screams as he drops the joystick and leaps to his feet.

Dex does the same while uttering a startled shout.

"What the hell!" was all Edwin can say as you look upon him through the mummy's hazy dead eyes.

Edwin! Call me a fag, will you? Punk me off in front of Kendra... will you?

You then remember that you cannot not speak with the mummy's atrophied larynx, so you put your thoughts aside and lumber towards Edwin.

"Shit!" Edwin exclaims. "That's... the fucking mummy from the exhibit! But it's alive now!"

You expected Billy and Dex to simply flee the clubhouse to get help, which was utterly pointless since it would only take you a moment to deal with Edwin. It would, however, get them out of your way and spare them from your wrath. Unfortunately, they do not fully succumb to terror and self-preservation as you had hoped.

"It's going after Edwin!" Dex shouted. "We gotta stop it!"

The boy picks up the wooden chair he was sitting on and smashes it over the mummy's back... *your* back. The article of furniture breaks into numerous pieces when it hits your mighty frame while causing you no injury or pain whatsoever. You are halted only in the sense that this blow causes you to turn around to see what had struck you.

"Stay out of this, fool!"

This time, Dex actually "hears" your psychic shout, due to the amulet's enhancement of your natural psychic faculties and your much more determined focus.

You backhand Edwin's nervy cousin with your closed fist to slap him aside. The blow, however, strikes him with the force of a wrecking ball, and sends the boy flying against the firm wooden wall on the far side of the clubhouse. His body smashes into it with such force that it actually cracks the wood along with several of his bones. Dex bounces from the wall after slamming into it, and you see that he ceases moving after he hits the floor.

Should have stayed out of my way, fool.

"Oh god! Dex!" Edwin screamed as he grabs another chair and prepares to use it to defend himself against you.

In the meantime, Billy picks up a spare piece of thick lumber and strikes you with it. He is much shorter than you are while inhabiting the mummy's form, so he is only able to reach your right shoulder with the makeshift bludgeon. He nevertheless hit you several times, and though the youth is unable to actually hurt you, he does anger you with his temerity to stand in your way. Nebka inaudibly reminds you that he would never have tolerated any attempts at the obstruction of his goals from the peasants who were beneath him.

As Billy swung at you again, you almost casually swat the wooden board in half with a single swipe of your arm. You then promptly seize the teen by the throat with both hands. You lift him in the air as if he weighs mere ounces. His eyes bulge from their sockets and his tongue protrudes from his mouth as he begins copiously gagging.

"Don't do that! Don't you dare strike me! No one hurts me anymore!"

That psychic message is the last thing the hapless Billy "hears" in this lifetime as you angrily tighten the grip of your vice-like fingers while holding him suspended several feet off the floor. His gagging is soon followed by blood flowing out of his mouth. Within seconds it also begins oozing out of his eyes like streams of thick scarlet tears as the orbs completely pop out of their sockets. After one last choking sound, Billy's body goes still, and you let it drop to the floor like a rag doll.

"Shit! No!" Edwin yelled as he hurls the chair at you and attempts to run out the door you smashed to pieces.

You swat the chair aside as if it were a mere piece of paper with your left hand while quickly reaching out with your right one and grasp the fleeing Edwin by the back of the neck. You hoist him into the air and slam him against the wall, holding him up by the throat while you put your hideous, withered face just an inch from his own. You do not kill him immediately, though; you want him to *know* who was snuffing out his life.

"God, no! Don't do this!" he shouts as he futilely pounds on you with both fists.

You ignore his fruitless counterattack while you concentrate and focus your psychic abilities to project an image into his mind. You force the mummy's shriveled black lips into a parody of a smile as a mental image of your face – your *real* face – suddenly sears into Edwin's mind.

"Walt?" he said while coughing and gasping in your grip. "Walt, this is… you, isn't it? You're in there!"

You nod the mummy's head in confirmation while maintaining that hideous smile. "*You shouldn't have humiliated me, Edwin. You should have been one of my subjects, not one of Vance's.*"

You then smash his head into the thick wooden wall three times with great force. You doubt it took all three to kill him, since his skull was in pieces and the wall was awash with blood and brain matter by the second blow. But you felt that you are entitled to vent a little against someone who had so seriously wronged you.

As you let Edwin's lifeless body drop to the floor, you walk out of the clubhouse with a clumsy but triumphant stride. The deed was done, and Nebka is proud of you as you follow in his footsteps.

A short time after my altercation with the two gang members, Everett Williams was outside his Prospect Avenue home adjusting some of the Christmas lights strung around the upper perimeter of his front porch. He whistled a notable holiday carol to himself while working, as he refused to wait until the next day to replace two of the tiny white bulbs that had shorted out. It didn't matter to the nice but tough old dude that it was so late at night, nor that the wind chill factor made it seem as cold as the icy plains of Niflheim. It was the Christmas season, he enjoyed the holidays, and he wouldn't tolerate any visible imperfection in his celebration of it.

That was fortunate for me, but maybe not so fortunate for him. I hated to do this, especially so unannounced and so late at night, but I had no one else I could turn to for this. And the human part of my psyche was scared while the animal part simply wanted to hide behind some snowbank and wait for the full healing process that would expunge all the buckshot from my leg to carry itself out. I couldn't wait, though, because my human side had another life that I needed to get back to as quickly as possible.

So, I forced my human psyche to stay ascendant and I ended up in Everett's driveway, hidden behind his car, when I caught his scent and heard his distinctive whistling. I was thankful that I didn't have to ring his back doorbell… like this. That would have been just *too* weird.

"Everett… I need your help…" my gravelly voice called out to him from the darkness as I forced my partly lupine larynx to pronounce those words.

"Huh? What?" he said, dropping one of the small bulbs before he could properly insert it on the wire. "Who's there? If you be some wise ass playin' tricks with me…"

"No tricks. I… need help." I walked out from behind his car on four legs where the illumination of his Christmas lights let him see me in all my wolfen glory.

"Oh, it's you. I wondered when or if I would ever see you again… Mike."

My yellowish eyes opened wide. "You… know?"

"Yeah, I done figured it out. And I also know you ain't a total bad sort. You saved my life. What do you need?"

"My leg… hit with buckshot. Hurt. I need it taken out… before I go back to being… person."

"Yeah, that sounds like a problem, all right. Okay, you wait outside my backyard door and I'll go inside and let you in. Stay quiet for a short spell 'till I get there, alright?"

"O-kay."

A few minutes later, it certainly felt strange strolling on two legs, but with a slight limp, in a person's house while in werewolf form. But I trusted Everett after what we went through together during the Jack Pack's assault on Prospect Avenue last month. He should have been terrified of the furry wolf-like monster walking behind him in his front parlor, but he showed no sign of it. And he showed no lack of trust on his end either.

Everett had full faith I was the "good sort" he believed me to be. I needed him to keep thinking that, but even more importantly, I *wanted* him to feel that way about me. Because truth to tell, I respected him, and would continue doing so no matter what I had become.

"Jesus H.," he griped as he inspected my wounds. "I see 'bout two dozen pellets in your leg. Weird looking leg, too. It's hard to see through all that fur you got there, so I gotta snip some of it off. You got strong muscles, so it looks like the buckshot didn't go in too far. Either that, or the healing power you said you got already took care of most of the damage they caused. And it sorta pushed those pellets further out of your muscles."

"Can you… get them out?" I asked.

"Well, I was a medic in Vietnam, so let's see what I can do. I still got some of the equipment I had then. Never wanted to be without it after what I went through there, even if I'm now here. I'm gonna use some tweezers to get 'em out of you, so this may hurt a bit."

He removed the first pellet before I knew what he was doing.

"Grarrr!"

"Okay, okay, maybe it'll hurt more than just a bit. You gotta man up now, okay? Let me do what's got to be done."

"O-kay. I can… take it."

Whether I could or not, I had to give it my best shot. Not only for my sake, since I needed to get those pellets out before I reverted to human. But also for Everett's sake, because he was going out on a limb here to help me, and the least I could do was make it as easy as possible for him.

I continued grumbling in pain for the next ten minutes, but Everett worked fast and efficiently. In that span of time, the buckshot was completely removed.

"There, that's the last of 'em," he said. "I should bandage up these little cuts."

"No… need. Will heal up. Fast."

"That's fine and dandy, but I don't want you bleeding on my rug in the meantime. This towel is only gonna soak up so much. Do ya know how much these rugs cost, kid?"

"O-kay. Bandage… if you have to."

After he wrapped up my leg, he brewed some java on his Mr. Coffee and sat beside me as I lay sprawled on his spacious couch. He still showed no sign of fear, and I couldn't help but respect him all the more for that.

"I would offer you some of this, but I don't want you lappin' it out the cup with your tongue like a dog. I'll wait 'till you change back and have a human mouth again. 'Bout how long will that be, if I may ask?"

"Until leg… heals up enough. Give it about another… ten minutes."

"Alright. Lemme take another look at that leg." He inspected the bandages carefully. "Hrm, there's barely a spot of blood on the bandages. I think it's safe to take it off now."

Everett removed the gauze and checked the actual wounds. "Barely a mark there now. Does it hurt a lot when I press in on it like this?"

"No."

"Then maybe it's time? No offense meant, but I don't want you to go and shed on my couch. Bad enough I gotta vacuum up after my cat."

"I'll… change now."

I went through the concentration ritual, focusing on the image of a new moon. Everett looked at me in complete fascination as my body re-shaped itself right before his eyes, losing muscle mass and fur to their otherdimensional source, until finally the monster on his couch was replaced by the human form of young teen Mike Nero. As I was now bereft of my natural coat of fur, and wearing nothing but my stretchable gray shorts, I suddenly felt as if I was freezing my ass off.

"Geez, Everett, don't you pay the heat bill?" I wondered as I pulled a blanket over myself.

"Sure I do, kid. I just keep the thermo down low, so the bills don't get sky high. A guy's gotta save however he can, and if you live in Buffalo, you should be able to take the cold like an Eskimo."

"If you say so, man. I'll take that hot coffee now too, if you don't mind."

"I got the decanter heated up, so it's comin'. How does the leg feel?"

"It stings and tingles just a bit, but only a bit. My shoulder feels fine. Thank Fenris for the healing power of lycanthropy."

"Thank who for what?"

"Ah, never mind."

I took the mug of hot coffee by the handle as he handed it to me and sipped it slowly. I thought it was so cool that the ceramic cup had a *Galaxy Quest* logo on it, as it was one of my favorite TV shows of all time; in fact, it was nothing less than a sci-fi series from the '60s that made the genre what it is today.

"So, you're a *Galaxy Quest* fan too?"

"Sorta. That mug was a gift from my daughter. Now, I think you have a long story to tell me, but I'm not sure you got the time now. As young as you are, I'm guessin' you have a home somewhere and folks that are worried about you. Or… don't you?"

"I… do. And I'm sorry to put you in yet another difficult position, but, um… I'm gonna have to use your phone to call them and come up with an excuse as to why I won't be coming home tonight. I'll tell them I'm staying at my friend Greydon's house like I do sometimes on Fridays. It's a good thing I don't have to go to school again until Monday."

"You got school again on Monday? I figured you were on Christmas vacation or something."

"Nope, that doesn't start 'till the week after next."

"Okay, boy. Now you're gonna tell me what in Hell's name you were doin' gallivanting outside as a wolfman tonight, and gettin' yourself shot on top of it all?"

"It's a bit of a long story, Everett. I'll give you the short version of it before getting some sleep. Um, since I don't have any money or tokens, do you think you can give me a ride home in the morning?"

"I suppose I'll have to."

"And… do you have some clothing I can borrow?"

"Jesus H. Christ, kid!"

Yeah, I hated to impose on Everett so much, but I really didn't have any other choice. If he ever needed the power of the werewolf at his side, it would be there for him. That was all I could silently offer him in return for now, but it certainly was something.

In the meantime, I had to steel up the nerve to call home and let my mother know I was staying somewhere overnight that I actually wasn't. I could only hope that she and my stepdad wouldn't piss me off too much with their response. For their sake, more than mine.

"Hello?" my mother's voice answered with a combination of irritation and worry.

She must have known it would be me on the other line. You would think they had invented some caller identification technology or something (we should be so lucky!).

"Mother, it's me," I responded.

"Mike, where the hell are you?"

Now it starts.

"I'm calling from Greydon's house. We got caught up in some things, and he needs my support, so I'm gonna stay here for the night."

"What kind of 'things,' Mike? Are you two getting involved with drugs or some shit?"

Look who's talking. But I'd best not say that to my 'child of the '60s' mother. Unless she really pisses me off.

"No, Mother. We just ran into a few punks and had a fight."

"A fight with *who?* Did you run into that Paulie delinquent again?"

"No, you don't know these punks, Mother. They're from Greydon's 'hood."

"So, he got you into this?"

"No, it wasn't his fault!"

"Were either of you hurt?"

"Just a few bruises, not enough to keep us out of school on Monday. His mom is gonna give me a ride home tomorrow."

"You don't have a fucking change of clothes!"

"Greydon's gonna let me borrow some of his clothing."

"How? He's three times your goddamn size!"

"His sister shrunk some of his clothing really badly in the wash. Those will fit me perfectly."

With my peripheral vision I couldn't help noticing Everett covering his eyes and shaking his head over that one.

Then my mother's tirade continued. "You think this is a big joke, don't you, you little fuck?"

"Look, I stashed some clothes here in case I ever had to stay unexpectedly. I could swear I told you that before, didn't I? But anyways, I'll be fine for tomorrow."

"I want to know if you're alright!"

"I told you that I was."

"I want to hear it from someone else. Put Greydon's mother on the phone now!"

Shit. I have to take a chance and hope Everett plays it off well.

"His mother is working late. Only his grandfather is here."

"Then let me talk to him!"

I held the phone out to Everett, making sure to emphasize the situation. "Mr. Minter, sir, since *you're Greydon's grandfather* and your daughter – *his mom* – isn't home right now, my mother wants to talk to you."

"Are you serious?" he lip synched to me.

"Yes," I lip synched back with a frantic nodding of my head.

Everett threw his hands up to indicate his irritation and then grudgingly snatched the rotary's handset from me.

"Hi, Mrs. Nero, how are you tonight?" he said, coarsely trying to feign a happy mood and doing his best to sound "white."

"Mike said that he and your grandson got into a fight with some punks," my mother replied. "Are they hurt badly?"

"No, no, they are not, ma'am. I tended to them myself. I have some medical training from my time in Vietnam. They're fine and your son is welcome to stay the night. My daughter will see to it he gets home tomorrow afternoon."

"Are you sure he doesn't look all bruised up?"

"No, ma'am. Your boy just has a few minor lacerations."

"Those are puncture wounds! I know what 'lacerations' are, Mr. Minter. I'm a nurse!"

"Oh, he wasn't stabbed any. Just lacerations of the minor sort. I believe he may have gotten hisself knocked into a pricker brush or something."

"In the snow? I think my husband Frank and I should drive over and bring him home."

"Well, that would be your right, ma'am. But he really is welcome to stay. And my grandson could use the shoulder. He's been crying all night."

"Greydon? *Crying?*"

"Oh, yeah! He's really a big baby when it comes down to it. Can't even deal with a simple black eye. He should have fought in the war, like I did!"

"My husband fought in the war too."

"Did he? Well, then he knows his stepson is with someone who understands what it's like to really go through some heavy shit."

At this point I was motioning strongly for Everett to politely seal the deal and hang up the phone. He swatted his index finger to his pursed lips several times to signify that he was shushing me.

"Well... I guess it's okay for tonight then," my mother decided, "if you say he isn't hurt. But he's going to get his ass whipped when he gets home tomorrow. And I want you to make sure that he comes home no later than noon, Mr. Minter."

"Consider his welcome overstayed after that, Mrs. Nero."

"That's Mrs. *Landers,* sir."

"Oh, my apologies, Mrs. Landers, ma'am."

"Just make sure he gets home by noon tomorrow, okay, Mr. Minter?"

"Thy will be done, ma'am."

I smirked at Everett's slick Biblical quote as he hung up the phone without saying "goodbye," indicating that my mother had done so first.

Damn, I am so not looking forward to going home tomorrow. And I'm going to need to do some serious *hunting soon to work this tension off.*

Everett then sauntered over to me and stuck his long stubby index finger in my face. "Boy, I should whip your pale little ass *for your mom* instead of just looking forward to her doin' it tomorrow."

Though my first inclination was to get angry back at him, my respect and gratitude for this cool older dude took me in a different direction.

I grabbed his extended finger and shook it gently. "I really appreciate your help tonight, Everett. You're practically the only friend I have. And you're also like the dad or grandad I wish I had."

The man's slightly wrinkled features suddenly softened a bit as he put his hand down and replied.

"Hey, don't you be givin' me any nightmares about the might've beens, boy! You're *more* than a handful as a friend, let alone any damn son or grandkid. Now… get yourself some sleep, 'cause you gotta wake up when the alarm goes off at 11, and I gotta get you home by the crack of noon. I'll… get the spare clothing I have for you ready."

I grinned at his deprecating humor. "You make the most of those few hours of sleep you're stuck with because of me too, old man," I replied with full sarcasm.

"Hah! I hope my alarm clock scares the shit outta you when it goes off. 'Night, kid!"

"And *you* better hope that I stopped peeing in my sleep a long time ago! *Hah!"*

"Boy, don't even think of emptyin' that bladder unless you're standing in front of a proper toilet! That flimsy ol' couch of mine might not look like much, but it's what I have, and I got too little patience with you right now as it is. Goodnight, Mike!""

"Goodnight, John-boy!"

After that final display of banter, my friend and host went to prepare things for me, much as my grandmother and mother used to do during somewhat happier times in my early childhood. A wave of comfy nostalgia washed over me as I laid back on the bumpy couch pillow and did my best to get as much sleep as possible before the morning.

***

Captain Jean Rogen was doing her best to show some consideration for Dex's condition as she stood over his hospital bed that cold Sunday morning attempting to interview him. The sixteen-year-old was swathed in bandages almost from head to foot, with one arm and one leg in casts that were elevated with straps. In a horrible case of irony, he now actually resembled the very entity that put him in this state.

The boy seemed to move in and out of consciousness due to his fractured skull and the heavy amount of opioids he was being intravenously fed to help keep the physical pain at bay.

Still, she had a job to do, which happened to be taking a very dangerous murderer off the streets.

"Dex," she said softly but firmly, "are you awake?"

She then noticed under the bandages that his right eye was swollen shut and a bulging purple bruise protruded like a small melon just below it on his cheek bone. His one good eye opened slowly when she spoke to him. The only sound she could hear was the incessant beeping of the heart monitor, which lent an eerie ambience to the room.

"I'm Captain Rogen," she continued. "I know you've been through a lot, but I want to personally ask you some questions about who did this to you, your cousin, and the other young man who was with you."

"Edwin…" he said through swollen lips and a few loosened teeth. "Is he…?"

Rogen went silent for a few seconds. "So, nobody told you? Idiots. Listen, I'm not going to coddle you, no matter what state you're in. Edwin is gone, and so is the young man, Billy Taylor, who was with the two of you at the time. They were killed by the same individual who did this to you. I want you to tell me who it was and help us get him behind bars so he can't hurt anyone else."

Dex's one good eye closed tightly. "Edwin… no. I tried to protect him…"

"I know you did. You're a very brave young man, and I need you to be brave again in dealing with this as best you can. You can help by telling me who did this to the three of you."

"Mummy…"

"I'm sorry, but your mom isn't at the hospital right now. I'm sure she'll be here to see you later, though."

"No… not mom. It was… mummy. *A* mummy."

"Dex, what are you trying to say? Please calm down and speak clearly. What do you mean, 'it was a mummy?'"

"Bandaged… horrible, wrinkled face. Big… real big. And real strong. I couldn't stop him, Captain. I *couldn't* stop him. And now, Edwin is…"

Dex coughed a few times and seemed to have a spasm. Then his one good eye closed.

"Dex…? Dex, are you still with me?"

Out like a fucking light. I can't push him any further now, not in his condition. The guilt is killing him worse than his injuries, so I should probably tell his doctor to get a psychiatrist up here to help him. As for the report, I'll just have to go with what I was able to get from him now. He said he saw… a mummy?

I was thankful to get to school on time the following Monday morning courtesy of a quick ride from Everett. We had finally exchanged phone numbers before he took me home Saturday afternoon, and I was twice thankful to officially have him in my corner.

I quietly called Everett for a ride because I ended up oversleeping that morning. The fights I had with my mother over the weekend over Friday night drained more of my strength than the bullet wounds I took that evening. So, yeah, I was really wiped out that morning.

Luckily, I still made it to school with just a smidge of time to spare. As I raced towards my locker, I did my best to ignore all the pointing and jeering I was receiving due to the out-of-style bell-bottom pants (an unfortunate birthday gift from my grandmother) that I had hurriedly thrown on that morning since I was in such a rush. It was unfortunate that these people couldn't know how they were making themselves potential targets of my fangs and claws by doing that.

When I finally turned the corner to the corridor where my locker was located, my collar was suddenly snagged by a strong arm and I was pushed up against the wall. It was none other than one of the greatest threats I had ever known: Principal Johnson. Just my luck I had to literally run afoul of him yet again while breaking his sacred rule about sprinting in the halls.

Shit.

"What did I tell you about running in the halls, young man?" he screamed in my face like a drill sergeant who had just caught a recruit sneaking a donut into the barracks. "What did I tell you about breaking my rules?"

"Not to do it, sir?" I practically stammered.

"And yet you did it anyway! How dare you violate the rules that maintain order in this school! And after I had already warned you about it! You can expect a letter being sent home to your parents, whom I will request to meet with me in my office to determine the consequences, both in this school and at your home. Now, go and get ready for your first class!"

The exalted one once again gave me a whack me on the ass to punish me via a combo of physical pain and public humiliation. And of course, the impending homosexual jokes could write themselves.

I seriously need to kill that man. Let's see him slap my ass and embarrass me like that after the werewolf rips off his fingers and shoves them down his throat. Or up his nostrils! Or up his ass!

And just like the last time that happened, Al Jenning, the bane of my existence who so happened to have been assigned a locker uncomfortably close to mine, was present to witness the spectacle.

"You're such a retard, man," Al remarked, as if he were on Johnson's side when he actually hated the guy as much as anyone else. But of course, he was on *anyone's* side if they happened to be going against me at the time.

"You probably enjoyed watching him do that again, so you're welcome," I retorted.

"You're the faggot, not me! A faggot and a retard! You should be in the rump class, not my homeroom."

By that point, Al had stepped right in my face. Or, more specifically regarding the much taller guy, my eyes were staring into this torso.

"And what's up with those pants?" he continued. "Did the Good Will have a clear-out sale? Did you put those pants on layaway there six months ago?"

I had now had enough. He was lucky I didn't have my knife on me. Still, I now made a definite decision that he was next on the werewolf's nocturnal target list. I also considered head-butting him or sinking my teeth into his arm again. As of that moment, however, I resorted to a one-liner comeback I knew he wouldn't like.

"I heard your momma is on a different sort of 'layaway' right now. The word is that she's pretty good, too. I'm sorry she almost choked to death last time, though."

Al looked around to make sure that no teachers, let alone Mr. Johnson or our nefarious hall monitor Mr. Woodman, were around. Once he determined the coast was clear, he pushed me up against the locker.

"You're dead, fag."

I gritted my teeth in a snarling expression as my temper began to flare. My next thought was not of a head-butt or biting into his arm, as I had done a few weeks ago. This time, I was going to bite the tip of his nose clean off.

"Go ahead, try and bite me again, you fucking animal!" Al baited. "You just try it. I'll have ten people waiting outside for you when classes let out."

Little did the idiot realize that I was entirely in the mood to comply with his request no matter his threats.

Before either of us could make another move, however, a soft feminine hand with tannish-brown skin and long fingernails painted red with black polka dots grasped my opponent's wrist.

"You lay off of him, Al," Kendra Calloway said in a soft but serious voice. "He's only half your size, and he didn't start with you."

"Stay out of this, Kendra," Al demanded. "Did you hear what he said about my mother?"

"He doesn't even know your mother, Al! So, his remark didn't mean anything, and he was only defending himself after you attacked him first. Now move on and let this go, okay?"

Al stared at the stunningly attractive girl for several seconds with a dumbstruck expression. But as she had both the looks and popularity among the student body, and was an upper classman to boot, he relented.

"Why are you defending this little wimp, Kendra?"

"Because you didn't need to be picking on him again. So, just leave him alone, okay?"

After glaring at her angrily for a few seconds, Al turned and stormed off. He knew that he was "outgunned" by a popular girl from the upper high school classes of the magnet school.

"Wow, thank you, Kendra," I said, both genuinely appreciative of such an exceedingly rare intervention on my behalf and rather smitten with her general awesomeness.

"Don't worry about it. Al is actually an okay guy, but he can get stupid sometimes. Are you alright?"

"He never shows any of that 'okay-ness' to me. And I'm fine, thanks. No need to worry about me. I can handle that asshole."

I could scarcely believe that Kendra was talking to me! It was at least as exciting as if Monica Mainfield herself had suddenly started speaking to me. I felt as if I were actually *somebody*.

"That's not the point, Mike. I've seen him harass you once too often, and today… well, I'm just not in the mood to look the other way."

Could it be? Or, is it too good to be true?

"Thank you for stepping up for me, Kendra. How about I pay you back by getting you a cheeseburger and a Dr. Fizz after school?"

"Um, okay, I guess."

Wow, I think I've heard more enthusiasm from people who were asked to identify a body at the morgue. Maybe I should have kept my mouth shut.

"I mean…" she tried to clarify her ambivalence, only to suddenly break into tears. "I'm so sorry. You know, I really could use someone to talk to."

"What's wrong?"

"My friend Edwin… he was murdered last Friday. Did you hear about it on the news?"

"I didn't, but then again I was… out all weekend. I'm really sorry."

"It was awful. It happened in his clubhouse. Vance and I would have been there if we hadn't decided to go to the Vermillion Room at the last minute instead. Edwin's friend Billy and his cousin Dex were hanging out there playing Atari with him. Dex didn't die, but he was really smashed up and he's at least temporarily paralyzed. I have no idea if he's in any shape to tell the police much."

"How many attackers were involved? Was it gang-related? The Red Dragons, or even the State Boys, maybe?"

"From what I heard, it was just one guy. Edwin wasn't involved in that gang shit. And no gun or knife was used; they were just… battered. That psycho broke his way in, because the door was smashed to pieces. I'm not sure how he could have done that, because it was a heavy wooden door and Edwin always kept it bolt-locked."

"Wow."

This incident sounds really strange. Apparently one guy was strong enough to do that to three guys without a gun? And to smash through a heavy wooden door that was bolt-locked? I'm not sure if even I could do that in wolfen form. Could it be that a certain werewolf now has another competitor for alpha predator of this city? As if the Jack Dog wasn't enough!

"Vance is really hurting over it. That's why he didn't come to school today. It… sounds a lot like the murder that happened at the museum, where I'm doing a study class on Egyptology."

"Okay, I did hear about that one. And you think what happened to Edwin and those other two is connected to what happened to that security guard at the museum?"

"Yea."

Kendra nervously adjusted her leg warmers before pulling a hanky from her purse and wiping her eyes. She was upset, seeing as how fidgety she was being. I couldn't help feeling bad for her, even if this did put a damper on getting to know her better. She was a junior in high school, though, so… that was probably not gonna happen anyway.

And again, those murders sounded really weird. Something, call it a sixth sense or whatever, was telling me that I should learn more about them. I realized that whoever – or whatever – was behind them may have eventually factored into my mission. I wondered if there was some common denominator between the murder at the museum and what happened to that Edwin.

"Okay, after school you have my shoulder. Along with a cheeseburger and a Dr. Fizz."

"Alright, thanks. I hope this doesn't sound strange, me hanging with you when we only know each other so casually."

"Nope, it's okay. That's how a… friendship starts, right?"

"Yea, it is. Let me be the one to treat you to that cheeseburger and soda, though, okay?"

"Don't worry, I have a good ten bucks on me."

"I insist."

"That would be embarrassing, though. A girl doesn't pick up the tab for a guy."

"Welcome to the '80s, bro. And it shouldn't matter anyway because it's the least I can do, and it's not like we're going on a date."

"Touché."

Okay, a hot junior like Kendra is not going to like me in that way. I get that. But… she's always been rather nice to me. I can't just forget that. And she is rather easy on the eyes, soooo… no harm in being seen with her, right? Maybe Monica will get jealous. Yea, mmhmm. But one can always have the fantasy when the reality sucks, right?

"But listen, I need to stop at the museum for a short lecture first. You can come with me if you don't need to get home too soon. I can show you the exhibit while we're there."

Hmmm…

"Yup, I'd like to see it, so that sounds groovy."

"Um, okay. But we should get to class before Mr. Woodman or Mr. Johnson sees us still talking in the hallway."

"I have no problem with skipping math because I suck at it anyway. English is my thing."

"Yea, it shows with that funky vocabulary of yours. But anyway, I don't suck at any class, so I need to attend them all. I'll meet you in front of the museum at four. There's a burger place right down the street from it, too. Do you know where the Buffalo Museum of Antiquities is, and can you get to it easily?"

"I do, and I can. I'll just get off the cheese at an earlier stop that happens to be just one block from it."

"I thought you weren't allowed to get off at any stop but the one where you're picked up in the morning."

"I didn't say we were allowed to. I just said that I'm going to. I'll meet you at the museum."

"Okay. Just don't get in trouble over me."

"How many guys don't get in trouble over a pretty girl at one time or another?"

She frowned. Kendra obviously wasn't in the mood to handle my poor excuses for either humor or flirtations."

"Sorry. Uncool of me."

"It's okay." She sniffled again, and I couldn't help feeling bad for her.

"Alright, see you there. Don't miss class on account of me."

I do want to find out about those murders and see if there is any connection with the museum. I'm no sleuth, but maybe I can spot something that the police haven't yet.

In the meantime, I can hide out in the TV/journalism room to avoid math, and I doubt Mrs. Linksy will even notice that I'm not there.

I also need to figure out the best time and place to introduce Al and maybe even Mr. Johnson to my more savage side. And the TV/journalism room is the perfect place to do some thinking… and planning. I can't wait to draw more blood from the assholes in the world.

So, I met Kendra outside the museum as promised. It was unlike a girl, especially a pretty one, not to stand me up. My respect for her went up another few notches as a result (several, actually).

She quickly ushered me out of the cold and inside the building, where she wanted me to see the Egyptian exhibit her class was studying for early college credits. College… I made a mental note that I needed to go there myself in a few years.

We soon reached the wing where the exhibit of the pharaoh Nebka was on display after having just been re-opened following the murder of that security guard. I guess the museum had too much time and money invested in this display from an ancient and admittedly really cool civilization to keep it closed for long.

The first thing I saw was the extremely tall and fearsome-looking mummy of Nebka standing lifeless in the open sarcophagus. Surrounding him were numerous artifacts that were recently excavated from his tomb in the deserts of Cairo.

I noticed more than that, however. I could somehow feel strange and disconcerting mystical energies coming from the exhibit – not only from the artifacts but also, and particularly, from the mummy. Maybe having recently become a lycanthrope using shamanistic magick, and beginning a personal study of the occult, made me more sensitive to these forces. Whatever the case, I could feel the flow of these energies washing over me, and I didn't like the sensation at all. There was something seriously *wrong* about this exhibit.

"Hey, Kendra," a young man's voice came from behind us.

I turned to see an older teen, only slightly taller than me, with brown skin and really frizzed out hair. He wore funky round bifocals and was thin and frail-looking, almost like a textbook example of a nerd. Those strange energies appeared to be emanating from him as well.

"Oh! Walt!" Kendra said with a start. "I didn't know you would be here!"

"Yeah, after the investigation ended, my internship was renewed," he explained. Then he looked at me and gave me the same type of odd, "sorting out" expression I had initially given him. "So, who is this, Kendra? Do you have a little brother you never told me about?"

She giggled. "No, Mike is just a friend."

Walt glared at me. "A friend, huh?"

Now visibly uncomfortable, Kendra tried to break the tension with a sociable introduction. "I should introduce you two. Mike, this is Walt. He's a guy I know from the neighborhood. Walt, this is Mike, a lower classman who attends Woodlawn with me."

Walt and I shook hands, both of us putting on fake smiles and instinctively sizing each other up.

"Yeah, I'm just some guy she knows from the 'hood," Walt said with an acid bite.

Kendra sighed. "Oh, Walt, I didn't mean it that way…"

"So, you're a bona fide friend of hers, huh, Mike?" he asked me.

"Yup, I guess I'm just lucky to have that level of status with her," I quipped in response, hoping to offset the friction and irritate Walt (as if I could somehow accomplish both at once).

He just glared at me again through those big round spectacles. I gave him a similar stare in return.

"Walt," Kendra suddenly said, sobbing as she did so. "Did you… hear?"

"Hear what?" he asked.

"I guess you didn't, then," she said through tear-stained eyes. "Edwin… was killed on Friday. It happened at his clubhouse, where he was hanging out with was his friend Billy and his cousin Dex."

"Seriously? My gods, that's horrible," Walt replied with a matter-of-fact tone that didn't sound to me like either shock or grief.

I found myself almost distracted from the traumatizing news that Kendra just gave us when I heard that Walt uses "my gods" – plural, just like I do – instead of "my god" in deference to Christianity's monotheistic "God." I realized that his internship at the museum exhibit must not be just a hobby – he must really be in spiritual alignment with the Egyptian deities, much as I am with the Norse.

"What happened at the clubhouse?" Walt queried to the dejected Kendra.

"Some psychotic asshole broke in and brutally beat down all three of them."

She was unable to say any more beyond that before covering her face with her hands and breaking into tears again.

"I'm so sorry, Kendra," Walt said as he put his arms around her in an embrace she didn't reciprocate. "But it's going to be okay. I'll be there for you to help you through this."

This guy obviously has the hots for her. She also very obviously doesn't *have the hots for him. Which means Walt probably doesn't like that 'pretty boy' Vance very much, since Kendra seems to have a thing for him. Do dickheads like Vance have any idea how lucky they are?*

Of course, that made me wonder about a few things.

Walt does intern work for this exhibit, which has a mummy and all sorts of ancient Egyptian relics from a pharaoh's tomb with intense negative mystical energy flowing out of it – the same type I sense around Walt himself. As I understand it, Vance was a good friend of Edwin, the guy who got pulverized by some psycho this past weekend. The murder of that security guard right before that occurred here in the museum, and specifically in the section hosting this exhibit.

Hmmm...

Before I could muse any further, Kendra broke away from Walt's overly tight embrace, obviously not comfortable with it. "I... appreciate you being there for me, Walt."

"Not a problem," he replied as he grabbed a pad and pencil from a nearby desk. "In fact, I'm going to give you my phone number, so you can call me anytime you need to talk, and..."

"That's sweet of you," she interrupted, "but I've been talking to Vance a lot already. This whole thing hit him hard, so we've been helping each other sort this out."

"Oh, yeah... Vance," Walt said bleakly.

Yup, I thought so. Dude must be as jealous of Vance as I am. Much more, in fact!

"Well, it was nice to see you," Kendra lamented to Walt, "but I just wanted to pick some stuff up here and show Mike the exhibit real quick. We're going down the street to get a burger so he can lend me a shoulder."

Walt seemed to tense up. "Well, that's nice of you, Mike."

"I thought so too," I said with a bite of sarcasm.

"But I told you I would always be there for you too, Kendra," Walt quickly noted. "So, since the exhibit is closing in just a few minutes, how about I go get a burger with you two? I mean, two shoulders are better than one, and it's not like there's any reason you would accept Mike's shoulder but not my own, right?"

"Maybe mine is less scrawny and holds up a bit better," I hissed with a grin.

The look Walt gave me back was anything but mirthful. Once again, I gave him the same stare in return.

"Mike..." Kendra admonished me gently. Then she sighed in resignation. "I guess you're right, Walt. You can come with us."

"Yes, please do come along, Walt," I added. "I would be interested to hear a lot more about this exhibit and anything you might know about ancient Egypt in general. I do think the subject is really interesting. And you're an expert, isn't that right, man?"

"Yes," he replied. "As a matter of fact, I am."

"Then let's talk about it over lunch," I said.

I actually didn't consider Walt inviting himself on my pseudo-date with Kendra to be all that terrible a thing. I figured that by talking to him, it would be interesting to see what I could learn about the relics from the Nebka exhibit... and about *him* personally.

Okay, I have to admit that I totally anticipated the experience at Yum's to go poorly between me and Walt. After all, we did start out as antagonistic rivals for the attention of Kendra. However, that was before I had come to accept that a hot and popular upperclassman was not going to have goo-goo eyes for me. It was also before the conversation we had at the coffee shop, where Walt and I came to realize that we were pretty much kindred spirits.

"So, your internship puts you in charge of that Egyptian exhibit at the museum?" I queried to Walt across the table where the three of us sat devouring burgers and sipping cocoa.

"The one dedicated to King Nebka the pharaoh, yeah," Walt replied. "Are you into Egyptology, Mike?"

"I'm into a lot of interesting things of that sort," I noted.

Walt looked at me quizzically as he sipped his cinnamon-laced chocolate drink. "'Of that sort?' Elaborate, maybe?"

"Anything to do with… the unusual," I responded. "Things from outside of everyday common knowledge and understanding: the occult, UFOs, magick, ESP, etc. All of that shit."

"Very interesting," Walt decided with a grin. "Are you familiar with the alleged Egyptian knowledge of acoustics for engineering purposes and their technique of tethering one's consciousness to the material plane after the physical body had expired?"

"I've read some material on that," I answered. "Egypt was a really cool civilization. There are many known societies in the past that developed all sorts of interesting knowledge that is lost or considered to be just fantasy now. As an example…"

"Um, guys," Kendra suddenly interjected as she buried her face in her hands. "I'm still not feeling so good after what happened to Edwin. I figured we could talk about that."

Walt and I took the hint, along with remembering the real reason we were supposed to be at the coffee shop with her.

"Aww, I'm sorry, Kendra," I said with sincerity. "We just got caught up in things."

"Yes," Walt agreed while putting his right hand on Kendra's shoulder. "I'm sorry, too. I really am concerned, and I'm here for you."

She flinched to shrug Walt's hand off her.

Geez. Poor dude, I thought. *But I have to admit that I feel even worse for Kendra, and for more than just having to deal with Walt's unreciprocated interest.*

"Look, Kendra, what happened to Edwin wasn't your fault," I said.

"Of course, it wasn't," Walt added. "It was Edwin's own fault. With his behavior, he obviously hurt and pissed off one too many people."

Kendra took her hands off her sobbing face and looked directly at Walt. Her light brown eyes, though swollen red from crying, did nothing to take away from her pretty features. The tone that came out of her mouth next was anything but pretty, though.

"Walt!" she exclaimed. "What the fuck's the matter with you? He was murdered!"

Walt seemed to be taken aback by her outburst. Me, I was more taken aback by the fact that he was taken aback in the first place, if that made sense.

"I'm sorry, Kendra," he replied. "I shouldn't have put it that way. I just didn't want you to take the blame yourself. It's not as if there was anything you could have done about it. I didn't mean to upset you, though. I actually care about you a lot."

He gently put his hand on one of hers, after which she quickly tore it away from his touch. Walt looked quite angry and embarrassed, but thankfully resisted the temptation to make anything of it.

"Stop, Walt," she said. "This is not the time for that, okay?"

"Not the time for what?" he asked. "Doesn't it help to know that you have someone who cares about you like I do?"

Whoa, I thought. *I feel like I'm a fly on the wall at a very private and awkward party. And it's getting as awkward for me as it is for them. Some non-divine intervention is required.*

"Walt," I interrupted, "I think Kendra is just really upset right now. She isn't responding to anything like she normally would. Maybe you should – that is, *we* should…"

Before I could finish the suggestion, I was suddenly hit in the face by a hurled, rolled-up napkin. I turned in that direction to see the ugly, grinning face of Paulie Dano, a nasty kid about two years my senior who had lived around the block from me for years. Alongside him were a couple of his partners-in-bullying, Ramus Edwards and Ne-ne Vasquez.

The former was almost as tall as Paulie, towering above me. He had a head of matted blonde hair, and his slight pot belly was the only thing that marred his impressive physique.

As for Ne-ne, he had classic dark Hispanic features with a beak-like nose that tarnished his attractiveness. He actually stood an inch *shorter* than me with a wiry build, but his strength and natural street fighting acumen were something to be reckoned with.

"Look who's here… in *our* coffee shop," Paulie said as he walked over to the table. "I'm not surprised to see a faggot like Mike sitting with a guy who looks like another piece of fruit, but what's the girl doing there with them?"

"Yeah, man," Ne-ne responded with a beam that showed off a mouth full of crooked teeth. "She's out of place with them. She should be hanging with *us* instead. Ha ha."

Oh no, not him. And just my luck he'd be with two of his dickhead cronies.

"Excuse me," Walt said with an angry expression while lowering his glasses. "I'm guessing that these guys are not friends of yours, Mike."

"What was your first hint?" I asked sarcastically.

"Why would we be friends with a fag?" Paulie said. "And why would *you* be friends with one?"

"Yeah," Ramus agreed. "Are you two gonna suck each other off once you leave here?"

"While you *maricones* are busy with each other, your friend there can come with us," Ne-ne stated while nodding towards Kendra. "She ain't doing you two no good, and vice-versa. Heh."

To my surprise, Walt was glaring at Paulie's crew with the same fierce expression I was, as if we were in on a little secret known to the two of us alone. I began wondering about Walt again, and he had likely started having similar suspicions about me. We both knew that look, and what it tended to entail. Moreover, we each sensed some unusual energies around the other.

Of course, it was Kendra who interceded with the heat of a blazing firebrand.

"You assholes had better cut the shit, or I'm going to tell Vinnie at the counter and get your asses kicked out. This is Vinnie's shop, *not* yours." She then stood up and got in Paulie's face despite standing a few inches shorter. "Hell, maybe I'll kick your ass myself."

"What's going on over there?" Vinnie shouted from behind the cash register. "Are you kids behaving?"

"Yeah, we're behaving, Vinnie," Paulie shouted back. "The three of us are just gonna get the usual and then we're outta here."

"Then come and cash out, and leave those kids alone," Vinnie said.

I had just come *thisclose* to losing my temper. I continued looking Paulie, Ramus, and Ne-ne in the face with defiant rage as they approached the counter, paid their bill, and left with their mochas. Walt was doing the same, and so was Kendra. I rarely had anyone, let alone a girl, stand up for me like that. She was really starting to act like a friend.

"Assholes…" Kendra lamented almost under her breath as she sat down again.

"I can agree," Walt noted. "Those ignorant poltroons need to feel superior to others. So, they insult and belittle those they perceive as weaker so they can come off as the alpha. Just like that archeology professor Billington from the university that tried downgrading me during my first day lecturing on the exhibit."

"Oh, come on now, Walt," Kendra said. "Dr. Billington isn't all that bad. He can be a hard ass, yea, but he's like that with all of us. No one should take it too personal when he gets all high and mighty on them."

Walt put his mug down on the surface of the table hard enough to cause it to shake before giving his indignant response. 'Not all that bad?' Kendra, you shouldn't be defending a bully like that. He went out of his way to make me look bad in front of the tour group, including the members of your class. He can't stand seeing anyone in the spotlight other than himself."

"I've met the type!" I responded with a laugh as I sipped my plain chocolate cocoa.

"I don't think you're being totally fair, Walt," Kendra insisted. "And I'm not sure it's a good comparison. Those punks were being assholes to people who were minding their own business. Dr. Billington was in a professional position. Even though I admit he can get a bit too blunt at times, he was simply giving what he considered a legitimate opinion in his own way of communicating."

"Really, Kendra?" was Walt's next response, as he struggled to keep his tone to an amicable volume.

Uh-oh. I don't like where this is going, I mused to myself. *Should I step in before it gets totally volcanic?*

"That professor you seem to worship is no better than those three punks you got kicked out of here," Walt continued. "They just lack his illustrious degree and respectable job, so he gets the free pass from you that they didn't. Don't excuse his behavior because he happens to be a bully with a PhD and a professional job."

"Walt, calm down, okay?" Kendra said. "I just don't think it was the same type of situation as this…"

"Sure, you didn't," Walt spat acerbically. "People always make some sort of excuse to treat bullies and haughty poltroons as if they are 'cool'… and those whom they step on as deserving of such abusive behavior."

I really wanted to tell Walt to simmer down and let this go, for fear he was going to lose any degree of respect Kendra may have had for him. But I just couldn't help being really sympathetic to what he was saying.

I mean, I didn't see what went down at the tour lecture, but from what I gathered, that professor was really disrespectful to Walt right in front of Kendra and a group of other people. Was it any wonder that he was so pissed? Why couldn't people like that Billington consider these things before just opening their mouths?

Meanwhile, Walt just kept on going.

"It's funny that I didn't see the curator of the museum step in and kick Billington out for his obnoxious behavior towards me like Vinnie did with those punks who harassed us. And I certainly didn't see you stand up and insist on it either, Kendra.

"I guess you just find Billington more appealing than me because he's this handsome, worldly, and cool professor with a big degree, hefty paycheck, and lofty reputation. The whole world would be better off without people like those punks... and Billington. I should have some words with him before this night is over."

By that point, Kendra had had enough. "What? Are you serious, Walt? How could you say that about anyone, after what happened to Edwin? And after a security guard who worked at the museum you're doing your internship at was murdered? What the hell is the matter with you?"

Walt again seemed to be taken by surprise, and the tension in the air was bearing down on our table like a pressure cooker.

Finally, the perpetually awkward and embarrassed Walt found a few words. "Kendra, I didn't mean..."

"Look," she interrupted, "this is just not a good day for me, and I don't need this shit! I'm out of here!"

Kendra threw the coin she owed for her share (which she insisted on paying for herself) of the lunch down on the table. She then stood up and began storming toward the door.

"Kendra!" Walt shouted after her as he also stood up. "I'm really sorry! I was only speaking my mind, just like you said Billington was. I didn't mean..."

Now I had to intervene. I stood up and gently blocked Walt's attempt to chase after her.

"Dude, let *me* try and fix this, okay? She's a bit too pissed at you right now. You'll only make it worse."

He gritted his teeth for a moment. "Alright. Just tell her I'm very sorry, and..."

"I got you covered," I said as I sprinted for the door.

"Hey, kid, are you gonna pay for your order?" Vinnie hollered as he saw me running out.

"I'll be right back, Vinnie!" I replied hastily. "Walt's gonna stay 'til I'm back so you don't think we're trying to hornswoggle you."

"You better not, kid—" was the last I heard of Vinnie's thick Brooklyn-born accent before I temporarily exited the place.

"Kendra!" I shouted as I caught up with her before she walked too far away from the shop. "Listen up..."

She turned to me and began leaking tears again. "Don't make excuses for him, Mike! I tried to be nice to Walt, but I just can't stand him hanging around me all the time, and..."

"Look, he doesn't mean to be, yanno, difficult or clingy. In case it wasn't obvious, the dude is hopelessly in love with you and thinks you're even more awesome than Diana Ross and Sheena Easton combined. But everyone is always mean to him. He's hurting a lot inside, so he just doesn't know how to express himself right.

"I know he comes off bad to you, but I can relate to his side of the situation. I respect how you feel, believe me. But I know how he feels too. So, is it possible to, yanno... forgive him?"

I actually found myself struggling not to shed tears along with Kendra. She was a tough girl, but not without a lot of compassion. She took both of my hands, and her touch felt refreshingly warm despite the chill winter air.

"Mike… I know, okay? I'm sorry for what guys like you and Walt have to go through. But… I can't feel the same way about him as he does for me. And… I can't lie to him and let him think there's any possibility of something between us. I don't think he's a bad person deep down… and neither are you, Mike. Maybe I can forgive him, but I can't deal with this right now. But after what he said about Edwin and Dr. Billington when he *knows* what I just went through…"

Kendra sniffled, held back more tears, and forged on with the impassioned spiel.

"Look, I just can't right now, okay? All I would end up doing is leading him on unintentionally. And right now, you're honestly better for him as company than I am. You understand him in a way that I'm just not capable of. Go back to him and tell him I forgive him, but right now, I need to go and find other support for myself. In the meantime, you provide the support for Walt. Okay?"

I nodded quietly. She gave me a quick hug and then headed for the bus stop at the end of the corner, determined to use her school pass for a free ride before the 6 PM time limit expired. I headed back into the shop, where I smiled and waved at Vinnie.

"See, I'm back! And I'll take care of the check now, as promised."

Vinnie just grumbled and nodded.

As Walt and I paid the check and departed the shop, I did my best to console him. The fact was, I *did* understand what he was dealing with, just as I understood why Kendra needed to get away from the situation.

"Look, man," I told him as we walked up the snow-covered street while the biting wind and flying snow drifts whipped at us. "Kendra says she forgives you. She's just very upset right now. And… well, she just doesn't have any special feelings for you. So, it makes her feel sort of nervous instead of happy when you show her how much you like her. That's why you need to cut back on that. I'm sorry, guy, but that's the way it is."

Walt gritted his teeth again. "Of course, she doesn't like me! She likes Vance because he's the 'cool' one! She probably likes that Billington poltroon for the same reason!"

"Calm down, man, I know how it feels and I don't handle it well either. I've not only been there so many times before, but I'm there right now. There's this girl at school… well, a few of them actually, but mainly Monica.

"She doesn't feel the same for me; actually, she thinks I'm a total nerd. All the nice-looking, popular guys she hangs with treat me like shit in front of her. I… want to *kill them* when they do that. It's really jive when something like this happens, but I want you to know that you're not alone in having to deal with it."

"Thank you. Honestly, Mike. But, you know, Kendra might like me more if those ignoramuses didn't make me look bad in front of her. Just as you said those guys make you look in front of that Monica girl. I really *do* need to have some words with Billington."

For some reason, I felt a chill down my spine when he said that… not because of the December wind hitting me in every direction but due to the way that Walt expressed those words. And this is *me* telling you that, mind you. I shrugged the chill feeling off as some of that whipping winter wind momentarily getting through the protection of my coat and continued the conversation.

"Don't let that college professor get to you, okay? And don't worry about Paulie and his two fellow poltroons – love that word, by the way! – because I'll deal with them."

"Do you want some help?"

"Huh? Um, no. But thanks just the same, ha ha."

"How do you plan to deal with them then?"

I seriously wanted to tell him the truth about me for a moment. But I decided against it, for now. Hel[1], I hadn't even told Greydon yet, and he was the closest thing I had to a best friend at the time. Also, it's not like I could let Walt tag along for my hunt anyway, right?

"Let me worry about that, okay?"

He looked at me suspiciously through the thick lenses of his bifocals. They made his eyes look much larger than they actually were and gave his already mousy appearance a boost of creepiness that did him no favors.

"If you say so, Mike. In the meantime… well, how about we exchange phone numbers and keep in touch? Seeing as how we understand each other, I think we should be friends."

"Sounds good to me. Do you got a pen?"

"I always have a pen on me. You never know when you might need to take notes. Do you have any paper?"

"Of course. I always steal some napkins from any restaurant I visit for no particular reason."

The numbers were exchanged, and I turned and headed in the opposite direction, telling Walt that's where the bus stop I needed was located.

It was still daylight, so transforming into wolfen form would be a bitch. Hence, I needed to haul ass if I wanted to catch up to Paulie and his cronies before they made it to their respective homes. I had their scents in my nose, and in a short time, I would have their blood in my mouth.

As Walt headed down the other side of the block, he had a look of grim determination on his countenance and one thought flashing through his troubled mind.

Billington. When I told Kendra and Mike I would have words with you tonight… I meant it. Even if I can only deliver them telepathically as I crush the life out of you.

As you can imagine, it's a lot more difficult for a werewolf to follow a spoor in human form than in his lupine mode. So, if I didn't want to lose Paulie's scent, I had to find a relatively warm place where I could safely store my coat, shirt, sneakers, socks, and those awful bell-bottom pants – which held what little money I had left –so I could attempt the transformation in the daylight. I did it before during my battle with the Jack Pack a few weeks ago, but this time it would not take place under duress with the adrenaline and extreme emotion borne of desperation to help things along. So, it would take a bit of work.

I knew it was the waxing moon and transforming was easier during that time, up to, and particularly on the three nights per month of the full moon. I had to keep practicing, though, since I didn't want to be in any way dependent on the phases of the moon for my transformations

---

[1] Yup, Mike totally meant 'Hel' with a single 'l' there – as in short for Hellheim, the Norse realm of the dead, and not the Christian 'Hell!'

– or other time-specific factors – like the cursed lycanthropes do. The latter are saddled with involuntary transformations during the nights of the full moon, so the time-specific factor is to be expected for most of them – as is their typical lack of control of their wolfen forms.

As a shamanistic werewolf, however, I should have complete control over the changes, and the majority of my actions while in that form. That is supposed to come with the territory when you take on the power of the lycanthrope via your own volition.

I quickly located a Doublemeat Palace I was familiar with, which I knew via a past act of elementary school mischief to have a small heating vent with an unscrewed screen located in the men's crapper. The vent's screen was, of course, detached without the knowledge of the restaurant's administration a few years back, courtesy of me and my friend Jon D'Angelo, so we could have a secret place to stash things. Long story. Anyway, it was perfect for what I needed now to try and initiate a daytime transformation.

With the small bathroom door locked, I stripped down to my stretchable gray shorts and hid my clothing in the vent. Thank Odin, the screen was still unbolted! What I had to do next was the really difficult part: not only to initiate the transformation in the day when I wasn't under duress, but to slip out of the bathroom and exit the restaurant in lupine form without being seen. It would be possible, given the speed and natural stealth I had in that form, but still a challenge. Luckily, the wind was really blowing outside, so the whirling snow would give me some degree of cover once I left the joint.

So, I went through the usual ritual, which in retrospect can be described as follows.

First, I mentally focused on the image of the full moon with the growling face of Fenris the wolf god superimposed on it. I called upon the latter's energies along with the power of Odin, the All-Father of the Norse deities and patron god of the berserkers and mixed them with the potent lunar energies of the near-full moon (or, as much of it as I could draw down during the day). I utilized all the will power and visualization skills I had thus far learned in my fledgling studies of the mystic arts to focus these energies into a very specific end goal; to tap into a specific set of forces. I thought about Paulie and his cronies, focusing my anger towards them into a compelling emotional force to give the procedure the final boost of energy it required to get through the daylight barrier.

As before, the daytime transformation took several minutes. And needless to say, it was quite uncomfortable for one's bones, muscles, and organs to re-align themselves over that duration even when they were partially (and temporarily) converted into ethereal matter. The latter conversion happens to ensure the change is both possible (such as accruing that additional mass from an otherworldly source) and non-fatal. It was quite a rush, and it took considerable effort to make no sound louder than simple whimpering from the discomfort; but in the end, it happened.

A werewolf now stood in one of the Doublemeat Palace's bathrooms.

My now ultra-keen hearing could detect neither heartbeat nor footfalls directly outside the restroom door. Luckily, that meant no one was impatiently waiting outside to use the john. I unlocked the door with my roughly human-shaped hands and peeked out. Only two customers were at the counter, and two more were sitting and eating at one of the more distant tables. No one present had any need to pay attention to the bathroom door. Hence, the coast was as clear as it was going to get.

When my enhanced senses determined the moment was just right, I dashed out of the bathroom on all fours and quickly exited the door leading out of the restaurant. Only one person was on his way into the place when I ran outside, and he jumped back with a startled, "Whoa!"

I was moving so fast, and disappeared down the block so quickly, it's likely that the poor sap had no idea what he had actually seen. I figured he would make up a good story for whoever he told later, though.

I swiftly picked up the trail of Paulie's scent and tracked him down several blocks. It was late afternoon, with darkness fast approaching, and I knew he rarely spent the quarter required to take the bus home. He reserved most of his bigger coins for video games and preferred to walk everywhere so the city was aware that it had the honor of his arrogant presence.

It was just late enough and cold enough that there weren't too many people around. There was also a sufficient number of huge snowbanks, parked vehicles, and alleys to give me cover when moving at such speed. Of course, that is why moving about in a snowy environment was a big advantage for a lycanthrope. Since we were in the Christmas season, the houses and business establishments across the city were decorated with bright lights and colorful Santa imagery. It was a beautiful sight to admire, but nothing related to beauty or aesthetic admiration was on my partly feral mind at the time.

After less than fifteen minutes, Paulie's scent became strong. I turned the block to find myself on the familiar grounds of Porter Avenue and there he was walking with Ne-ne. It seemed the third malcontent of the crew, Ramus, had since parted ways with them. *Shit.* Still, I knew I could always save him for a subsequent hunt[2]. It was going to be an early Christmas for me, and a very bad holiday season for Paulie and Ne-ne.

Of course, it was just my luck that an inconvenient coincidence was now rearing its horrid head. Either that, or the trickster deity Loki decided to do what he does best when I happen to be his target.

As it turned out, right around the corner from where Paulie and Ne-ne were now walking, was none other than Officer Lamar Middleton. He wasn't in uniform, and technically on sick leave (thanks to me), but he was still carrying his gun. The cop was in the process of parking his car in front of a nearby donut shop to avail himself of the free pastries and coffee that lawmen were provided there, even when off-duty.

I came up behind Paulie and Ne-ne just before they turned the corner. Only one other person was out and about, an older man walking across the street. Paulie was pointing at the man and poking fun at him, telling his friend that the guy was probably gay or something, as I rushed toward them like a train out of Helheim.

Naturally, I headed for Paulie first. He screamed as I stood up on two legs, grabbed him from behind in my powerful clawed hands, and lifted him in the air as if he were a sack of feathers. I slammed him on the icy concrete and smushed his face down into a few inches of snow to muffle his shouting. I then tore through the back of his heavy winter coat with the talons of my other hand, easily slicing through the down-lined jacket to the flesh underneath. I growled excitedly as I watched small spurts of blood flow out the horrid wound I tore into his upper back like several miniature fountains of scarlet fondue.

However, Paulie wasn't the only one screaming. Ne-ne was shrieking like a banshee himself, not to mention uttering what was probably a string of curse words in Spanish. He ran around the corner in a panic while I ripped into his friend, leaving Paulie with scars both physical and emotional that would likely never fully heal.

---

[2] To find out what happened on that subsequent Christmas Eve hunt for Ramus, see the short story "Nero: A Holiday Haunting," available as a free download on the Wild Hunt Press public group on Facebook. It shall soon be provided as a free bonus for the paperback version of this book!

Ne-ne swerved right onto the next block, running as fast as his short but athletic form would take him, screeching, "It's the wolfman! It's the wolfman!"

My seemingly trickster-induced luck continued as Ne-ne dashed in front of the donut shop just in time to almost literally run into Lamar. The off-duty cop ignored the pain in his still-injured shoulder as he snagged the panic-stricken young man by the collar of his coat.

"Did you say 'wolfman,' kid?" Lamar asked the terrified teen.

"Yeah, man!" Ne-ne shouted back. "Let go of me! The fucking wolfman! It's killing my friend or some shit like that!"

Lamar could tell this boy's terror was real. That was fully confirmed a few seconds later when my furry self, having finished ripping into Paulie, left him bleeding in the snow to pursue Ne-ne around the corner. I stopped a few feet from the teen and stood up to my full height of well over six feet to find myself muzzle-to-face with a certain cop I was acquainted with; one who had vowed to make a rug out of my hairy hide.

"Shit!" Lamar yelled as he pushed Ne-ne onto the snow. "Get down, kid!"

"I'm down, I'm down, man!" Ne-ne hollered as he buried his face in the white frost.

The cop managed to draw his gun in the literal blink of an eye, coaxing a snarl from my inhuman throat. Damn, he was fast – and despite the injury I had personally inflicted on him a week earlier!

Before I could rush Lamar, he managed to get off a shot. The lead projectile penetrated the left bicep just below my armpit, passing clear through the limb. I growled in anger and pain as I moved forward and struck the cop in his sternum with my open palm. The blow sent him clear off his feet and down onto the icy pavement a few yards away. Thankfully, he was momentarily stunned.

"Damn you!" I bellowed at him in the gravelly voice produced by my partly wolfen larynx. "I *hate* getting shot!"

I then got down on all fours and took off as fast as I could, ignoring the pain of the rapidly-healing gunshot wound in my left arm. I was at least thankful that this time the bullet passed clean through without burying itself in my epidermis. I was heading back towards the Doublemeat Palace where I stashed my clothing, and I was in no rush to recover it since that one in particular was open 24 hours.

That bastard ass fuzz! He's lucky I didn't cut him open instead of just smacking him. I hope he pulled a disc when he hit the fucking pavement!

Behind me the hard-boiled cop was quick to recover. No sooner was he back on his feet than he retrieved his piece and pulled the trembling Ne-ne back on his feet with one strong heave of his good arm.

"What, what?" the boy shouted in a state of panic. "Is it gone? Is it gone?"

"Yeah, it's gone for now," Lamar answered.

"But Paulie! The wolfman tore up Paulie!"

"Bring me to him!"

Ne-ne ran back around the corner with the armed Officer Middleton mere inches behind him. It was there that the cop saw Paulie laying on the sidewalk, writhing and moaning in agony while the gaping wound on his back stained the snow around him a bright red.

"Aw, man! Paulie!" Ne-ne yelled as he ran to his friend.

"Son of a bitch," Lamar said to himself as he looked at the bloody sight before him.

Fuck this sick leave shit! I'm going to call dispatch right now. That werewolf is going down.

Kendra Calloway walked gloomily up the front steps of the home she shared with her parents and older brother, her eyes still bloodshot and puffy from crying. That situation was not destined to end any time soon as she opened the front door to find an unexpected guest sitting on the couch alongside her parents waiting for her return home.

"Sweetheart," her mom said gently, "this is Captain Jean Rogen of the Buffalo Police. She's… looking into what happened to Edwin and wanted to ask you a few questions. If you're up to it, that is."

"Nice to meet you, Kendra," Rogen said as she stood up and shook the girl's hand before she could respond to her mother's concern. "Your parents were telling me what a smart girl you are. I figure that you're likely a strong girl too, and that you would indeed be up to this."

"We also told you that this incident hit her really hard, Captain," Mr. Calloway noted. "She was almost at the clubhouse during the time that… whole thing happened."

"Which I think would be all the more reason she would want me to catch the perp responsible," Rogen remarked.

Kendra disliked the captain's brusque, in-your-face way of conducting herself as much as her parents did, but it also made the lawwoman seem like the type who was determined to get results even if she must ruffle a few feathers in the process. And she did indeed want whoever killed Edwin and those other people in such a brutal fashion off the streets.

"I'm fine with answering the questions, Captain," she said.

"Good girl," Rogen replied. "First up, let me tell you what led me to question you, Kendra. When I got a statement from Edwin's cousin Dex, the sole survivor of that incident, he claimed the attacker – whom he saw up close and very personal – was a most unusual individual."

"How do you mean?" Kendra queried.

"Let's just say that the description he provided fit that of someone you would expect to find at a… history museum. I'm sure you know that a security guard at the Buffalo Museum of Antiquities was recently killed by an unseen individual whom we believe is the same perp that killed your friend. And it also happens to be a place that you, Edwin, and other students in your circle of peers were likewise associated with – even if in a more or less peripheral sense."

Kendra's eyes opened extremely wide when she heard those words. It almost looked as if she were in shock.

"Sweetheart…?" her mom inquired.

"Based on that stunned silence of yours, Kendra, I'm guessing that I struck a major nerve with that info," Rogen stated firmly. "So, let me be blunt. Do you know something, or at least *suspect* a specific someone, who is connected to that museum that I should know about?"

Mr. Calloway stood up. "Captain, are you accusing my daughter of something? Because, if you are…"

"No, sir, I am not!" Rogen was quick to interject. "I am asking her – asking *you,* Kendra – if the simple association you and Edwin had with the Buffalo Museum of Antiquities may have caused you to witness something suspicious. Someone that may have wanted to cause harm to Edwin, and possibly to others in your circle."

"Oh god… no." Kendra buried her face in her hands, went down on her knees, and began crying again.

Both her parents came to her side and gave her supportive embraces.

"Kendra," Rogen said, "take a few minutes to compose yourself and please tell me who you suspect. This is very important and will not only allow us to catch the individual who took your friend's life but also to prevent other incidents like this from happening."

"Back off please, Captain," Mr. Calloway insisted.

"Walter…" Kendra muttered through the hands cupped over her face.

Rogen stepped a bit closer and turned her ear in Kendra's direction. "'Walter,' did you say? Walter who?"

Kendra finally forced herself into a semblance of composure while holding both her parents closely. She then began telling her suspicions, praying to God that she was not throwing accusations that were in error.

"Walter Lavelle. He's… a boy from this neighborhood. He has recently been working as an intern at the museum for the Egyptian exhibit of King Nebka."

"Do you mean *that* Walter, Kendra?" her father asked. "The one who used to deliver papers here and seems to like you?"

"Yea, him, Dad," Kendra confirmed.

"But he's… this skinny drink of water," Mr. Calloway said. "He couldn't possibly have…"

"Honey, are you sure about this?" Mrs. Calloway queried resolutely but supportively.

"I'm sure, Mom," Kendra replied. "I think I am, at least."

"What makes you suspect him, Kendra?" Rogen questioned.

"He… *hated* Edwin," the young woman stated. "I think he was jealous of him, and this was at least partly over me. Walt may seem like a skinny wuss type, but he's… I don't think he's totally harmless like he seems. He's got a lot of pain and anger in him, and sometimes he acts like he's about to go over the deep end… if he hasn't already."

"When and where did you see Walter last?" Rogen asked.

"Um, just about an hour or so ago. I hung out with him and another friend, a younger kid named Mike Nero, who isn't associated with the museum, at Yum's – you know, that coffee shop near the museum? Well, Walt was acting really strange and bitter, and he was very upset after these three punks walked in there and called him and Mike names. I got them thrown out, but then he started saying bad things about Dr. Billington. You know, Dr. Kent Billington, the professor from Elmwood University who is our instructor for the Egyptology class at the museum. He said…"

Kendra trailed off and began sniffling.

"What did he say, Kendra?" Rogen asked.

"Oh, god," she sobbed. "Dr. Billington. Walt said he wanted to… have 'words' with him tonight. And the way he said it…"

Kendra's parents embraced her again. The look on Rogen's face was one of great alarm.

"Jesus Christ," she said. "Billington. Kendra, do you know if he would be in his office at the university or at home at this hour?"

"It's… it's Monday," Kendra said. "He has a late-night class there tonight that goes past 7 PM. So, he's always in his office past nine, just in case any of his students need to speak to him after class."

The police captain rushed to the front door. "Kendra, thank you for your courage here! Mr. and Mrs. Calloway, contact your daughter's school to arrange for grief counseling if she needs it. I have to leave now!"

Rogen jumped into her car and turned on the police radio attached to the front of the dashboard. "Dispatch! This is Captain Rogen! You need to send a unit to meet me over at the Elmwood University and get a Dr. Kent Billington in protective custody! As in, yesterday!"

In the meantime, Mr. and Mrs. Calloway helped their daughter back on her feet and to the couch, where she laid down.

"Sweetie, I'm going to make you some relaxing tea, okay?" her mom said.

Kendra simply nodded as her besieged mind moved onto other things. *Oh, Walt, you poor stupid bastard. Please don't have gone over the edge… even though I think you did. If you killed Edwin because of me, that makes all of this my fault! Mine!*

Then another realization sent her back on edge, much like Rogen had been a few minutes prior.

"Oh my god," she whispered aloud. "Vance! I gotta warn him!"

Kendra ran over to the phone and dialed Vance's number, straining to avoid sounding as near-hysterical as she was. The line was answered by his little sister.

"Janine, this is your brother Vance's friend, Kendra. Is he home? I need to talk to him right away!"

She listened to the response for a few seconds. "Okay, do you know where he is then?"

After another response, Kendra said, "Alright, I'll go there now. Thank you!"

Mrs. Calloway was very justifiably concerned to walk into the front room with the promised tea to find that Kendra had inexplicably departed the house. The woman felt as if her daughter was headed towards an extremely dangerous situation.

Unfortunately, she was correct.

There were three customers and two employees behind the cash registers at the Doublemeat Palace when I rushed back in. I managed to push the bathroom door open and get inside without any of them seeing me… only to immediately realize that I had broken the lock (hey, sometimes I don't know my own strength in lycanthrope form!). There I found myself standing before and looking down at some poor schmuck with his pants around his ankles and emptying the meat hose in the urinal.

Shit!

The unfortunate dude turned around, saw my hulking lupine figure towering over him, and his mouth opened so wide I thought his jawbone would crack. Within a second and a half I had the horrified gent pressed up against the wall with my furry hand covering his mouth to stifle his screams.

With my free hand I pressed my long, furry index finger over my muzzle and managed to utter a "Shhhh…" sound.

The man nodded his head frantically in compliance with my polite request. It was then I realized that I had so abruptly interrupted his business that he had peed all over my shaggy left leg.

Oh shit! My fur is already starting to stink! Now I gotta wash myself! Don't lose it, Nero…
this guy didn't do anything other than having to pee at the wrong place and the wrong time.

What really sucked about this situation was that I obviously couldn't change in front of that schmuck, and I had to wait before doing so until my arm had fully healed. I simply didn't want to risk reverting back to human with a half-healed bullet wound in my arm.

"Pull up pants… and get out of here," I ordered him as my extended snout full of razor-sharp teeth bared themselves in the man's face. "Don't… scream or say anything. Understand? Don't make me come out there… after you."

The man nodded his head even more frenetically than before. He quickly pulled up his pants scampered out of the bathroom, and exited the restaurant as unobtrusively as possible, all the while panting like an asthmatic having an attack.

I then turned on the water faucet full blast and pulled several of those dull brown paper towels from the wall dispenser. I soaked them under the stream and thoroughly cleaned off my soiled fur. Next, I then sat on the floor in front of the door so my great bulk blocked it from being opened (since the lock was now broken thanks to me). There I patiently waited for my arm to fully heal, which it managed to do in an impressively short time.

Following that, I initiated the mental steps for the counter-transformation-ritual and within seconds I had reverted to human. Once I was a seemingly normal teen again, I retrieved my clothing from where it was stashed in the heating vent and donned it before carefully replacing the loosened venting shaft. Once that was done, I nonchalantly walked out of the bathroom and departed the restaurant.

I was now headed home, and much like the werewolf's latest victims, I was going to get seriously chewed out.

The bus I took got me there within twenty minutes after I left the burger joint. It was too late to use my school pass by that time, but what the Hel; I usually kept a few spare tokens handy for that reason.

My arm still ached a bit, but the worst of it had healed up, so the residual pain was nothing my human form couldn't cope with. What would prove truly difficult to handle was the fact that my sometimes friend/sometimes foe Marcus Gekko was hanging around the house with my long-time friend Chuck Heino and my younger cousin Tish.

"Hey," Marcus said to me as he saw me approaching the house from the bus stop. "Did you hear what happened to Paulie?"

"Not until you tell me," I lied in response.

"Mmmhmm. Right," he said with a look of angry suspicion. "Paulie, a guy who picked on you for the longest time, gets torn up by the West Side Wolfman on a night when you were out, just a short time before you get home. And you were out past, what, seven o'clock?"

"He really thinks it's you, Mike!" Tish added.

"Geez, that again?" I scoffed with a roll of the eyes. "I was hanging with friends at Yum's today; one of them was upset and needed a shoulder. They saw me head towards the bus stop that takes me home."

"You were at Yum's?" Chuck queried with a snicker. "I heard only faggots go there. Who were those friends you went with?" He made a point to flutter his eyelids in an exaggerated "feminine" manner to extenuate his flippant insinuation.

"Hey, that place has really good cocoa!" Tish noted. "You don't gotta be a fag to like cocoa! Right?"

"Hey, don't start that shit now, man," I said to Chuck. "One of those friends was a girl."

"Was she a lezzie?" he asked with a snicker.

Before I could protest again, Marcus shifted back to the point he insisted on making. "You were out with friends at a fag place? Bullshit! I'm betting you were hunting down Paulie. I talked to Ne-ne about an hour ago; he was with Paulie at the time and saw the wolfman. It scared the shit out of him! He says he only survived because he took the gun from this cop the monster knocked down and shot it."

I just had to roll my eyes at Ne-ne's version of the story.

"And you believe all that?" I asked him.

"Look, I already saw the report on the *6:00 News,*" Marcus replied. "That was less than ninety minutes ago. I also happened to run into Paulie, Ramus, and Ne-ne just fifteen minutes before it happened, and they told me that they ran into you at the coffee shop and made fun of you and this other kid. I ended up walking home with Ramus after that, because Paulie and Ne-ne went down towards Porter instead. And that's when and where the wolf attack went down. It was less than a half hour after they saw you and started shit with you."

"So, what was Paulie and his boys doing at the fag shop?" Chuck queried, trying to bring the conversation back to a less-than-serious direction.

"I told you, it has really good cocoa there!" Tish again offered as an explanation. "Don't straight guys like cocoa? Or, are they not supposed to like it?"

"How do you know one of the Red Dragons didn't do it?" I asked Marcus, ignoring Chuck's remark and Tish's tirade. "Paulie and his crew get involved in all kinds of shit."

"I don't believe it was the gang," Marcus said. "Paulie was cool with them. It was *you.* Just like two months ago when you did the same thing to those other guys who used to pick on you. Why don't you admit it? It's obvious, man."

"So, are you the wolfman, Mike?" Chuck inquired in an only half-serious tone.

"Yea, is it you?" Tish seconded the question. "Have you been, like, biting people up and killing them and stuff?"

"It's *him,*" Marcus insisted while pointing directly at me.

"I think you've been watching too many episodes of *Fantasy Island,*" I said. "Or, have you been sniffing more than the usual amount of glue lately?"

Our exchange was then rudely but conveniently interrupted by an all-too familiar voice that reverberated from the top of the stairs at my house.

"Michael Alexander Nero! You get in here right now!"

It was my grandmother… now the shit was going to hit the fan as if it were blasted from a cannon.

"Do you know how worried sick your mother was over you?" was her next expected question.

"Yes, I know, you all still think I'm a little kid," I snapped back. "I was only hanging out with friends."

"Marcus thinks he's been biting people up again," Tish said.

"Shut up!" I replied before turning back to my grandmother. "I told you, I was only out with friends. They needed some support because of something bad that happened. We just lost track of the time. It can happen. Leave me alone now, okay?"

That was when my grandfather stepped outside, and in one of his infamous moods.

"You heard what you grandmother said!" he yelled. "Get the hell in here before I go down there and drag you in by the hair!"

That threat caused the animal side of my psyche to flare up, and I gnashed my teeth with a slight growl.

"Did you hear what he just did?" Marcus whispered to Chuck and Tish.

"He's only joshing you, dude," Chuck opined.

"He's gonna get in trouble now!" Tish said to belabor the obvious.

Since I didn't want my grandfather to go down there and make such an embarrassing scene, I walked up the porch to the hallway. "I'll go inside. Just don't put your hands on me, okay?"

"Shut up and get in here!" he said while grabbing me by the right arm – which was still somewhat tender from the bullet wound – and dragging me into the door.

Okay, I did warn him, so, I bit his arm and slapped it away from me.

"Ooop!" he yelped in pain. "That little animal bit me!"

My grandfather then demonstrated what being strong was when he grabbed me and effortlessly slammed me against the door. I went right down with the wind practically knocked out of me.

"Now, get up and get in there!" he said, pointing to the open door leading inside his house.

I kicked at him several times to startle him into moving away before jumping up and running off the porch. I shoved Marcus aside as I passed him to rush back towards the bus stop at the corner.

"Oh, for cripes sake, Michael!" my grandmother shouted to me. "You get the hell back here, now!" She then turned to her dangerously strong husband. "James, go after him! What if he doesn't come home tonight?"

"We should be so lucky," my grandad said before turning and walking back inside the house. "Maybe he'll end up at Father Baker's, where he belongs."

"I bet he's going to go out and attack someone else tonight," Marcus said to Chuck and Tish.

"Oh, come on now," Chuck replied.

"Seriously, man," Marcus retorted. "I know he's the wolfman. And I'm gonna prove it and do something about him before he kills one of us next."

***

Captain Jean Rogen was driving as fast as she could through the snow-and-slush-filled Elmwood Avenue to join the four-person unit she had requested to meet her at Buffalo's Elmwood University. She was well aware that Dr. Kent Billington's continued enjoyment of life depended on her getting to him before Walter Lavelle did.

The roads were slippery, and the blowing wind strained her windshield wipers' capacity to maintain adequate visibility, but that did not deter her haste. Having operated during Queen City winters for her entire career in law enforcement she had grown used to the necessity of combining caution with speed under inclement conditions. This was one of those times the tough-as-steel lawwoman needed it the most, particularly since she had to talk over the dispatch radio while driving.

"So, you're still at the Lavelle residence, Simmons?"

"Yes, Captain," Simmons replied over the crackling dispatch. "His father, who is a single parent bearing full custody of Walter, says his son is not there. The boy told his dad that he was going to the Buffalo Museum of Antiquities to do some extra studying for his internship. Evidently, the previous guard would break the rules to let him do that, and Walter claimed the new guard is doing the same."

"Son of a bitch."

"Captain?"

"Get two officers to the museum immediately! I don't care how thin we're stretched right now – Christmas, the gang activity, and that stupid ass wolfman be damned! I also want you to stay at the Lavelle residence until further notice in case Walter comes home. If he does, keep him there under guard… and let me know immediately, if you do! I'm almost at the university, so I need to go now!"

Pulling your thick winter coat around your body, you trek through the dark, seemingly lifeless campus of Elmwood University, Walter Lavelle. You carefully scan the spaces between the lingering cars in the parking lot to ensure that no one is out and about to spot you here.

Though your eyeglasses correct the irritating near-sightedness you have had to contend with since childhood, the blowing snow still makes it difficult to see anything clearly beyond about two dozen feet in front of you. Nevertheless, you have the satisfaction of knowing that this also worked to your advantage, as it would likewise be difficult for anyone to positively identify you from a distance under these conditions.

You also feel secure in the educated assumption that the cold December weather has made it less likely that too many people remain on campus after the last class had let out – or that any that any muggers were lurking about in the large, darkened parking lot.

It would seem I'm alone here. I had little doubt that an obsessive academic like Billington would maintain his late-night office hours despite weather conditions unfit even for the gods; in fact, he and his sycophant secretary Isabel are probably the only two people still on campus right now. It certainly wasn't hard to confirm he was there with a simple phone call to his office. I just wish I could have seen the look on his arrogant face when whoever called him had the temerity to hang up as soon as he picked up the phone and said, in that haughty Brit accent, "Dr. Billington speaking, how may I help you?"

You do your best to ignore the cold wind that assails your fragile human body despite your heavy winter attire while you find a secluded area near the building that houses Billington's office. Once you do so, you slip into the dark space and stand fully erect while concentrating your will into the amulet with its embedded red jewel around your neck. The power of Anubis and Wepwawet are called upon, further augmented by the energies of Ptah focused through a piece of the Jewel of Seven Stars.

Your physical body quickly exchanges places with the sarcophagus-bound mummy of Nebka, secure in its exhibit back at the museum. Your consciousness transfers into that of the giant bandaged cadaver as it changes physical locations with your human body. Your psyche now once again co-exists with the semi-dormant psyche of Nebka that remains an eternal prisoner of his specially embalmed corpse.

By now, Walter Lavelle, you have grown used to the strange feeling of molecular de-materialization accompanied by the sensation of your mind "floating" from one place to another that characterizes this amazing transference. You have also gained full command of the mummy's powerful muscle movement. Taking advantage of the increased quickness you now possess in this form, you direct the mummy into opening the door leading into the administrative building. It is there you know Billington's office to be located, just a few floors up from the ground level.

I can only hope that Isabel isn't there. I shouldn't have to kill her, too. She never wronged me in any way. But the way she sucks up to Billington like so many other girls, she probably is.

"Do not have sympathy for the peasantry beneath you," was the unsolicited advice of Nebka's consciousness you were forced to share this mighty bandaged form with. *"That will only make you weak, and it is not the way of a ruler of men, which I can help you become… as I once was."*

But there has to be some type of code we follow, right? Isn't that how kings are supposed to behave?

"Our first responsibility, little Walter, is in securing our own dominion. You know there are many who would be willing to take it from you at the first sign of weakness or distraction! Do not give consideration to their fragile, ephemeral lives. They are our subjects, not our friends or allies, and we forget that at our own peril."

But this is not the same world you ruled over, Nebka. A lot has changed over thousands of years…

"And, as I observe this strange new world through your eyes and memories, I have seen that much has also not *changed since my reign. Men still rule over other men, still demand tribute from those they stand above; to allow the peasantry only very limited access to the resources and comforts they command. The basic code that I lived under thousands of years ago still holds true in this world of yours. Heed my words if you want to acquire what is rightfully due to those of our station!"*

Okay…

What you are not aware of, Walter, was that several minutes earlier, Dr. Billington was about to have some visitors prior to your impending arrival.

***

At the time, the professor who was the target of the mummy's murderous hatred was casually receiving a cup of coffee. It was provided, as always, from his devoted secretary and former student, Isabel Valdez.

"I put two milligrams of creamer in it and a simple pinch of sugar, just how you like it," Isabel said proudly as she put the steaming mug down on the professor's disorganized desk.

"As ever, Isabel," the archeology instructor replied with a smile, "I can scarcely imagine what I would do without you."

I'd rather think about what you'd like to do with *me, Kent,* the young woman thought to herself. As ever, though, the professor was oblivious and non-receptive to her yearnings.

"It's my pleasure, Dr. Billington," was what she said aloud. "I guess it's just us here in the building tonight."

"So, it would seem. That is not a surprising development when you consider the nature of the weather outside. Hardly unusual for Buffalo this time of year, though."

"Wait… I hear a few people running up the stairs. Were you expecting a few students, Doctor?"

Billington puts down his mug and peered out his open office door with an expression of bewilderment. "No, I was not."

His surprise was exacerbated when four police officers rushed into his personal base of operations on campus.

"What is the meaning of this?" Billington demanded to know.

"Captain Rogen will explain," one of the officers, a woman named Delby, told him. "She's on her way up right behind us."

A moment later, as promised, Captain Jean Rogen entered the office, her arrival having almost precisely coincided with the unit of officers she called for.

"Dr. Billington, I presume?" the captain queried.

"Yes," he replied. "Captain Rogen?"

"Also, yes," she said. "Now, listen to me, and I'll answer the questions you obviously have. We believe you've been targeted by the same individual who killed the museum security guard and those kids at that backyard clubhouse. I gather you've heard about all this on the news?"

Isabel's eyes and mouth opened wide as her skin turned white as the snow accumulating outside the building.

'Yes, I heard about all that," the professor confirmed. "But why would that killer want me next? What do *I* have to do with any of what *he* has to do with?"

"We'll tell you what we know after we get you into protective custody," the captain replied. "You and this young lady need to leave here with us right now. I'm going to take you to your home and leave two officers there with you until this… person is in custody."

"Oh my god, Doctor," Isabel said, trembling as she struggled to process what was now transpiring.

"It's okay, dear," he responded. "We'll just do what the captain is asking, and everything will be fine. I still must demand a good explanation for all of this, as I have responsibilities both within and outside of this university."

"Yeah, yeah, I get that, Doctor," the captain retorted. "But that can come later, as we have to get you the hell out of here now…"

Unfortunately for them, Walter Lavelle would not allow them a departure free of incident…as the mummy had heard the words of these lawmen outside the office when he arrived on the third floor of the building.

Oh no, you nervously think to yourself, Walter Lavelle. *The police got here first! How could they have known? Maybe I should call this off…*

"No!" the mind of Nebka rumbles at you psychically. *"You must not let such fools stand in the way of your just retribution. They are pawns of the current ruling rabble, beneath your consideration. They mean to stop you and force you to endure the continued humiliation of your inferiors. How dare they stand in your way! Kill them all!"*

But...

"*Indecisiveness is for ineffectual fools, not a ruler of men! You have the power now! Use it! Use it so you can acquire more power still and become all that you are destined to be!*"

Yes, you're right!

Your goal, guided by the mind of Nebka, is to terminate those five police officers as quickly as possible. To that end, you grab a 300-pound metal desk in the center of the corridor with your bandaged hands and lift it in front of you as if it were a mere toy. You walk over to the open door of Billington's office, making haste to commit your intended act of savagery before they can fulfill their own plan to leave the building and depart the campus.

You move as silently as you can, but it was not quiet enough.

"Captain, do you hear something in the hallway?" another cop, Smith, asks.

Rogen and everyone else in the office turn to see your seven-foot-plus bandaged form hoisting the table over your head by the entrance at just the proper angle to use it as a weapon. All the lawmen draw their guns, but not quickly enough to fire before you hurl the lethal makeshift projectile.

The table sailed through the air, making it into the room where it struck one of the officers – a man named Bedowsky – directly on the left temple. He fired a shot wildly into the ceiling as his skull was split open. You hear Isabel scream. Then you see Billington, your true target, grab the curly-haired young woman in a protective embrace and push her to the far side of the office to give the remaining four officers room to move.

"Jesus Christ!" another officer, Cannon, yells. "Captain, will you look at that! It's a fucking mummy!"

"I can see that, you simp!" the captain bellows. "Well, what are you waiting for? Shoot the son of a bitch!"

The three officers follow their captain by taking two shots each at your hideous, towering form. The powerful animated corpse under your control stumbles backwards with the impact of the slugs that manage to hit you, a few in your chest and one in your right shoulder. They penetrate deep within your decaying flesh, but despite being startled by the impact, you feel no pain, and you suffer no actual injury. No blood seeps out of the bullet holes, but simply small wisps of dust.

"The bullets aren't stopping it!" Delby exclaims. "It's coming at us again, Captain!"

"Son of a bitch!" Rogen hollers as she fires another shot.

This time, her aim for your throat strikes true. The leaden slug tears through your now useless esophagus and the sheer force of it knocks you back a step. You are taken aback, and you choke up a puff of dust... but you remain uninjured. The dark lips on your withered face curl back to expose what remains of the mummy's sharpened, yellowed teeth in an expression that can be readily identified as pure rage.

"Oh shit!" Delby shouts.

"You three, get out your billy clubs and beat the fuck out of that thing!" Rogen commands. "I'm gonna get the professor and the girl out of here!"

"You heard the captain! Beat that sumbitch down!" Cannon barks in front of you as he and his two fellow officers brandish their nightsticks and pile on top of your much taller form.

They pummel you on your skull and limbs with their wooden bludgeons in a brutal, merciless fashion as Rogen motions to Billington and Isabel to follow her out of the room.

"*Do not allow this!*" Nebka yells into your mind.

I won't!

For several seconds, you buckle somewhat under the onslaught due to your natural learned expectation that severe pain and the shedding of blood will accompany such an attack – along with the fact that even your mighty unliving form has limits to how much force it can withstand. But you quickly realize that you can endure even so vicious an assault by three baton-wielding officers, at least long enough to act before they have the chance to do some actual, debilitating damage to your ancient anatomy.

You hurl one of your tightly wrapped fists at Cannon. You strike him in the head-on and your knuckles embed an inch into the bones and cartilage of his face. He dies instantly. When you withdraw your hand – covered with bits of blood and gore – the now faceless officer slumps down to the carpeted floor.

"Shit!" Delby yells again as she executes a change of tactics against you.

You now have the officer called Smith's throat in your hands and you hold him above you in mid-air as he struggles and gags… when Delby makes that unexpected move. She slams her billy club just below your right knee, hoping to cripple you with a broken fibula.

That proves ineffective, as you barely flinch while choking the life out of Smith with one hand. As you maximize your grip, the thumb of your left hand sinks into the flesh of his Adam's apple and his eyes bulge from their sockets. Seconds later, blood mixed with saliva dribbles out his mouth and stains the filthy wrappings around your hand a dull brown. You drop Smith's spent body to the floor after it goes limp in your grasp.

"Damn you!" Delby screams as she again switches tactics.

The new move entails slamming her billy club with all her might into the popliteal fossa area behind your knee joint. It succeeds in causing your leg to involuntarily bend forward, and you partially tumble to the carpet. You do not remain there for long, of course, as the valiant officer proves unable to deal you the crippling blow she hoped for; the nerves in your leg muscles are long dead and therefore not vulnerable to becoming inflamed.

However, the blow does knock you off-balance just long enough for her to run out of the office and join the captain as the latter is guiding your true target safely toward the stairway.

"You're gonna fucking pay for those cops you killed!" she hollers with intense conviction as she exits the room.

You rise back to your feet and storm out of the office in pursuit of your target and the lawmen who dared interfere with your retribution.

Just outside of your view, Delby catches up to Rogen near the stairway.

"The other three?" the captain asks with a grim expression.

Delby simply shakes her head.

"Oh my god!" Isabel utters through tears.

"We all know the chances we take, girl," Rogen says. "But they aren't gonna die in vain! Delby, take these civilians to the car and get them out of here! I'm gonna slow this bastard down some!"

"Captain, let me—"

"Don't argue, just do it!"

You hear the captain holler that command to Delby as you approach her from just a few feet away, Walter. You are now hot on their heels, as your Uncle Maurice would say.

"Come on, Isabel!" Billington tells his secretary as he grabs her by the arm and allows them to be hurriedly led down the stairs by Delby – and out of *your* grasp.

To your surprise, however, Captain Rogen stands her ground and points her piece at you again. How foolish could she be? It is only when you see where she is aiming that you realize, to your horror, that she may not be so foolish after all.

"Maybe I can't kill you, but let's see if I can blind your fucking ass!"

She fires a shot, but despite the shriveled nature of the mummy's body, its reaction time is as impressive as its strength. You manage, albeit barely, to raise your right arm in time to take the bullet in place of your right eye. You have no idea what a shot to the eyeballs will do to you, as you are yet uncertain if this mummy actually depends on its ocular organs for the equivalent of sight.

You thus likewise block her second shot toward the other eye, this time with your left arm. As before, the slug enters the desiccated flesh and bone but causes no pain or debilitating damage. You manage to exude a sound resembling a light moan from your shriveled larynx in place of the intended scream of rage as you reach towards Rogen, determined to do worse to her than what you did to the three officers that you had just pulverized.

Unfortunately, the captain has yet another plan in the making, one that her quick mind executes just before you can grab her skull and crush it like a melon as intended.

As you reach for Rogen, she suddenly produces a small Bic butane lighter and clicks its tiny metal lever with her thumb.

"Time to flick my Bic, asshole!"

A small but potent flame erupts from the lighter's nozzle and ignites the dry wrappings of your hand, with the flame quickly spreading up your forearm.

You open your blackened mouth widely in a soundless screaming gesture as your limb is sieged by an extremely uncomfortable sensation, one that is difficult to put into words but is highly equivalent to agonizing pain. You fall back from the captain as quickly as you can, making sure to put several feet of distance between you and the small but dangerous plume of flame.

"I'm glad I never gave up the old high school habit of carrying a cigarette lighter with me to thicken my mascara," you vaguely hear Rogen remark just before you see her take flight down the stairs.

"Snuff the flame!" Nebka's psychic voice screams at you. *"Snuff it swiftly, or all will be lost!"*

Thankfully, you spot a porcelain drinking fountain in the center of the hallway. You thrust your bandaged forearm over the spigot and turn the lever with your other hand. A stream of warm water flows outwards, dousing the flame before your limb can fully immolate. You examine the somewhat charred wrappings around your arm and hand, wriggling the fingers about to see if there is any loss of movement. You are satisfied that no serious damage was done, and the remnants of the horrific sensation caused by the flames rapidly fades to nil.

That... bitch! She ruined everything! Okay, maybe I'll have to wait before I can get Billington. But Vance was next on my list! He was actually above *Edwin on my list, but he wasn't at the clubhouse that night. I said I would get him later, though.*

I'm going to show Nebka that I have what it takes to be a ruler of men. I missed getting Vance before, but I know where he lives.

I'm going to kill him. Right now!

I can guess that I have no need to say how angry I was after my latest falling out with my grandfather. He always enjoyed humiliating me in front of my friends, and I really had to get the rage inside of me under control. The wolf that could be released was no longer just metaphorical.

Now that I was several blocks away from him, I needed to take a breather, maybe even go on the hunt. But hunt who? I still wanted to get Paulie's cohorts Ne-ne and Ramus, but I couldn't be certain they would be out in this freezing weather; especially not Ne-ne after I had already put the fear of the wolf in him.

I could possibly have picked up their scents and tracked them to their homes, but then what? Was I to break through the front door or leap through the kitchen window in dramatic fashion and terrify their families along with my target? If someone in their family tried to defend them, was I to hurt them too?

What if they had very young siblings who would bear witness to all of that? What if a neighbor heard something and called the police – and as luck would have it, there happened to be a squad car right around the block at the time? Was I to fight and injure the cops again, who were just doing their goddamned jobs? And maybe risk getting shot again too?

I had to consider all these things. I mean, okay, I was a monster, a predatory hunter out for revenge; I wasn't a nice guy. I understood that much about myself. But… how far should I let myself go? I hadn't even been able to get myself to actually kill anyone I managed to get my talons on thus far, and it's not because I didn't harbor the desire.

Why so many contradictions with me? What exactly did I become, and what exactly was I on the road to becoming? Were there different possibilities from this point?

My jumbled musings were interrupted when I realized that my wanderings had taken me down Plymouth Avenue, which is the neighborhood where both my newest friends Walt and Kendra lived. Did I do this subconsciously? I must have, as I saw Kendra around there a few times, and only learned earlier that day about Walt sharing the 'hood with her.

No sooner did I realize that when, sure enough, an obviously distraught Kendra walked out her front door and began running down her steps of her porch as if she had a serious purpose. I saw her from further down the block and called to her.

"Fancy meeting you a second time in one day, pretty lady."

"Mike?" She was obviously crying and in a state of near-hysteria when she turned around.

I ran over to her. "Kendra, what's wrong? You look really upset."

"It's… look, the police were just at my house. They… they think Walt is behind those killings. You know, the guard at the museum… and Edwin. And I think they're right."

I wanted to look surprised. I tried to look just a bit startled. But the truth is, I had some odd suspicions from earlier, based on things that I noticed. I had simply tried to downplay them in my mind until now. I was beginning to see a potential friend in Walt, and… well, I didn't want to believe this, but I couldn't deny that gut feeling.

"Kendra, are you sure?"

"I… think I am. And I think you think so too."

Oh, man, Walt.

"Well… if it's true, all we can do is wait for the cops to find some real evidence."

"No! Listen to me! Vance is in danger! Walt hates him more than he did Edwin, or anyone else for that matter! He kills everyone that he hates! What kind of person can hate others so much? *What kind?*"

For a second there, I looked down, unable to make eye contact with Kendra as I pondered her question.

"I've gotta warn Vance, Mike! But he isn't home! He's at this guy Zach's house, who lives a short distance away. I know where it is, and I have to go over there and warn Vance! I can't let him die because of me!"

"Kendra, wait! That's waaaayy too dangerous!"

"I don't care! It's all my fault that Walt hates Vance so much! And that he hated Edwin!"

"No, it isn't. It's no one's fault but his own. Listen, give me the address, and I'll go warn Vance. And maybe try to talk to Walt if I can find him. I'll let him know what this is doing to you."

"So that maybe he kills you next? I can't let you risk yourself for me, Mike. I won't have another death on my hands! Not another one!"

"It's my choice. And if you go, I'm gonna follow you there anyways. Okay? That's my choice. Not yours, or anyone else's. Whatever may happen to me, it's all on me alone. Okay?"

"I need to get there!"

That was the last thing she yelled before taking off for the place. As I promised, I was close behind. To be truthful, as much as Kendra was guilting herself over this, I don't think she wanted to go alone anyway. And could I have let her even if she did? I mean, she had always been really nice to me, and… well, I just couldn't let her deal with something like this alone. That's not what a friend would do, right?

As she said, the place Kendra was headed to was just a few blocks away from Vance's house. It seems he too needed someone to talk to over the loss of Edwin, and this Zach person was it. Luckily, we caught him there. Of course, Vance never liked me even though he barely knew me, so he simply ignored my presence and spoke to Kendra as we both walked him home.

"You can't go home, Vance," she pleaded. "You're in danger, and the rest of your family would be too if you go there! Let me talk to that police captain – Captain Rogen, I think her name is – and I'll have her get you and your family protection."

"Look, I know how freaked out you are about what happened to Edwin," Vance replied. "I am too. But, c'mon now, Walt is a skinny little faggot who probably couldn't kill an ant if he tried. The murderer can't be him! No gun or knife was used in the murders, and Edwin would've cream-ated that dickhead if he got in his face without a serious weapon in his hand."

"Vance, you don't understand," Kendra asserted. "There's… something about Walt; more to him than we know. He started getting really strange and over the edge after he got that internship at the museum, and there's something seriously fucked up about that Egyptian exhibit! It all started there somehow. Walt killed that guard before he killed Edwin!"

"That's several shovelfuls of bullshit, Kendra," Vance countered. "That kid just isn't physically capable of something like that, no matter how weird or demented his mind may be."

I had to admit to myself that I was having a hard time sympathizing with someone like Vance – and with Edwin, if he was anything like his friend.

They just sounded far too similar to the people who caused me the pain that led me down the path I was now on – the same path as (apparently) Walt. I know exactly how it feels from his side of things. At least Walt and I had logical reasons for hating and hurting the people we did. Vance and guys like my own worst bully Dean O'Sullivan had *no* good reason to hate and hurt us. I felt that maybe Kendra should have tried to understand Walt a bit more instead of talking like he alone is some type of demented monster. And if he is, it's only because other people made him that way. I mean, you reap what you sow, correct?

Still, I was not going to let Walt hurt her. Or even Vance, considering how Kendra felt about him.

As we headed in front of an alley on a dark, snow-capped street a block or two from Vance's house, I started getting that tingling sensation I felt when I was around Walt – as if he were radiating some type of energy, a force I couldn't understand that marked him as something more than he truly was.

The sensation became overwhelmingly strong as we passed in front of the alley… and a huge arm swathed in dirty bandages suddenly reached out of the darkness and grasped Vance by the throat. It lifted him into the air as if he were weightless and pulled him into the seclusion of the alleyway.

Kendra screamed in terror and fueled by a combo of instinct and concern she ran into the lane after them. I stepped in front of the alley's entrance and was astounded by the incredible sight that awaited me.

"Oh my god, it's the mummy!" I heard Kendra shout. "The mummy from the museum!"

As I looked through the blowing snow, I recognized it also: the mummy of Nebka, from the museum's Egyptian exhibit. The one where Walt was doing his internship! I saw the mummy when I went there, even if only briefly, but that one time was more than enough to recognize that horrible rag-covered thing.

So, now it all makes sense! Walt is somehow animating and controlling that mummy. He's making it stalk and kill people for him. How… familiar that sounds.

"Walt, I know you're controlling that thing somehow!" Kendra shrieked as she pounded on the mummy to no avail while he carried the struggling Vance further into the garbage-filled lane. "I know you can hear me! Please stop this! Don't do this again!"

The mummy gave her a casual shove, which was enough to send her flying against the side of a brick tenement that formed the right side of the alley. I knew he was in love with Kendra, but since she had rejected him, I also knew that must make him hate her too.

"Walt!" I shouted to the mummy. "It's me, Mike! If that's you controlling that thing, please let Vance go and talk to me, okay, bro? I know he did some jive shit to you, but he means a lot to Kendra; and she means a lot to you, so…"

The mummy turned and glared at me through hazy gray eyes. Suddenly, I reeled back as my mind was inundated by a "loud" psychic communication.

"Mike! Stay out of this! Go home! Please!"

Even though I "heard" those words in my head rather than my ears, it was in what my mind interpreted as Walt's voice. I also received an image of his human face overlayed on the "sound."

Geez, it really is him!

I now realized that Kendra was in grave danger. Whether I should or shouldn't be concerned about Vance was then beside the point for me. She cared about him, and she was nice to me. That was so rare, especially from a girl. As much as I sympathized with Walt, I believed that my decision was clear.

Since it was now evening under a waxing moon, it would be simple enough to initiate the change… and quickly. I took off my coat and kicked off my sneakers as I visualized an image of the full moon and drew down its lunar energies along with the power of Fenris. Unfortunately, I had no choice but to sacrifice the rest of my clothing, save for the stretchable gray gym shorts I had on under my blue jeans. When the transformation commenced, my expanding lupine body quickly tore them to shreds as if they were tissue paper.

In the thirty seconds or so that my metamorphosis required, the mummy had walked to the far end of the alley and pushed the still elevated and wriggling Vance against a mortar wall. Walt raised the mummy's huge, bundled fist, which was covered with the brownish stain of dried blood from a previous kill that night. His intention was obvious.

Before he could throw the fatal punch, however, the mummy suddenly found himself pushed away from the wall and smashed against the side of the apartment complex on the right of the alley by something large and heavy that hit him at high speed. The unexpected impact caused him to drop Vance on the snow-covered ground, where he grabbed his bruised throat and hacked incessantly. Kendra had just began stirring again, and she ran over to him.

Meanwhile, the mummy's ugly withered face and dull gray eyes looked quite astonished as he found himself held against the wall by a werewolf. That was me, of course.

"Walt… stop! Let's… talk," I managed to utter in a deep, scratchy voice.

Huh? What the hell? Walt thought to himself as he projected his psychically enhanced mind into the creature before him.

What he saw when he peered into the outer layers of my mind was an image of Mike Nero, his almost newest friend.

"Mike? This is you? Why am I not surprised to find out that you're the West Side Wolfman? I knew there was more to you than on the surface, just as you must have sensed it with me too."

Since we could talk through focused psychic projection as long as his mind was actively "touching" mine, I continued our communique along those lines. It was easier for me than to struggle doing so verbally while in lupine form.

"Walt," I said, *"that is enough. We have to talk this out. You can't hurt Kendra. She is a nice person."*

"Nice enough to take Vance's side over mine, right? She always cared about punks like him, but never me! They probably only wanted to use her, but I love her, Mike!"

"I know, man. But that doesn't mean someone will love you back in the same way. She tried to be nice, but sometimes guys like us are difficult to be nice to. I understand you, though, so let's talk."

"Maybe you really don't understand me, Mike! Look, the two of us each acquired great power! Those poltroons always thought they were better than us, but we're higher beings than they are. Together, we could make them pay for hurting us. As dangerous as we are alone, we could be invincible together! We could be rulers of men instead of garbage beneath their heels."

"I… hear you, man. But… I can't let you hurt Kendra, Walt. I'm… sorry, but I just can't."

"Then that means you took their side over mine too. That means you are my enemy, and now I'm going to hurt you along with them!"

Walt made good on his word a second later when he shoved me with such force that I went flying off his embalmed body to slam hard into the wall on the left side of the alley. The impact was brutal and even in my mighty lupine form I nearly had the wind knocked out of me. That mummy controlled by Walt was *seriously* strong. I could see that this was going to be a tough one.

As I was recovering from being stunned, Kendra managed to get a still choking Vance back on his feet. Unfortunately, Walt saw this and turned his rage-fueled attention back to them. This wave of strong emotions enabled him to project a psychic message to them in his "voice."

"Kendra! Why did you take that ingrate's side over mine? He doesn't care for you like I do!"

She was stopped in her tracks after being momentarily startled by the psychic torrent suddenly projected into her head.

"Walt? Then it *is* you in there! You're controlling the mummy somehow! Please stop doing this! I know you care about me, and if you do, please stop this craziness! Let me and Vance go!"

"But... you already betrayed my feelings for those stuck-up, entitled poltroons! You will go right to the police if I let you leave! I don't want to hurt you... I never wanted to hurt you, *of all people in this disgusting world, Kendra... but you hurt me in more ways than one! I have to do... what must be done before you hurt and betray me again!"*

"Vance, we gotta get out of here!" she shouted to her friend.

"This... thing killed Edwin," he said painfully through a severely bruised – but thankfully intact – larynx. "That little... faggot is controlling it? *Coughs* I'm gonna... kill him."

"We will see who kills who in a second, won't we, Vance?" the mummy projected directly into his target's mind as the bandaged abomination began trudging toward them again.

"Shit..." Vance muttered to himself as he received the psychic communication.

"Vance, run!" Kendra shouted as she pulled her stubborn friend by the arm.

That guy really is an asshole, I thought to myself as I fully recovered my senses.

Kendra finally got Vance to follow her, but the mummy was moving toward them fast. Their slowness due to the pain Vance was suffering from and the fact that they had to plod through a few inches of snow was hindering the two enough to make them an easy catch. Or, at least they would have been had I not rushed at Walt's giant bundled form on all fours like, well, a wolf out of Helheim.

I leapt through the air and slammed into my opponent again with as much force as my inertia enabled. This knocked the mummy off his feet and the two of us went rolling onto the ground, kicking up blankets of snow in every direction as we did so.

Kendra was smart enough to take full advantage of that to keep Vance and herself moving as fast as they could. They dashed out of the alley and up Plymouth Avenue towards the Marina Harbor.

In the meantime, I ripped and tore at the mummy's rotten flesh under the wrappings like the savage beast I now was. My goal was to try and tear that dirty gauze off him, hoping the ancient form beneath would collapse into dust without their preservative nature. I didn't know what this would do to Walt's mind, but I didn't have a choice; I had to fully release the animal side of my psyche to have a fighting chance of winning this squabble.

The mummy let out a few soft gurgles borne of pain, anger, or alarm – it didn't matter to me which of these was correct – as I tore whatever I could from the ancient corpse with a mad fury. Walt directed his mighty vessel to pound on me with a frenzy of blows in a desperate attempt to dislodge me before I could succeed. His first few strikes were painful but too wild to succeed in knocking me off. One of the succeeding blows, however, struck me clear in the side of the rib cage. That nasty haymaker felt as if it had managed to inflict a slight fracture. I howled in pain as he grabbed me by the mane of grayish fur atop my head with one arm and wrenched me off him.

The mummy hoisted me up by the scruff of my neck and smashed me up against the mortar wall a few feet away. Despite being thoroughly rattled, I was still able to retaliate with a vicious slash across his shriveled, parchment-like facial skin.

"Hrarr!" the bandaged creature managed to utter in response.

He then delivered a punch to the side of my ribs that worsened the previous fracture. I again howled in anguish as he slammed me down against the snow-covered concrete. That, too, did my splintered rib absolutely no favors.

"Mike, you forced me to do this! I won't let you betray me again!"

I was then knocked senseless with a powerful downward punch by both his fists at once. They hit like piledrivers, and my muzzle spit blood as the simultaneous blows landed. He then easily lifted my 400+-pound form and hurled me across the opposite side of the alley. I struck the hard wall with great force, and my vision went black as I then fell to the slushy ground beneath.

"You made me do this, Mike!" was the last thought in my mind – one externally projected by Walt – before the lights went out.

The mummy then turned and began to pursue Kendra and Vance towards the Marina Harbor on this cold winter night. The harbor was just under two miles away, but most kids in Buffalo knew a short cut that could take you there in about twenty minutes on foot if you kept moving quickly.

As for me, I could only lay on a carpet of snow, bleeding and defeated with all my senses forcibly switched off.

***

Captain Jean Rogen found herself speeding through the slippery streets for a second time in one night. In this instance she was heading back towards the Calloway residence.

"If you weren't my boss, Captain, I would give you a ticket right now," Delby said glibly.

"Look," the captain replied, "I know bad humor is just your way of dealing with… what we just dealt with, Delby. And I'm glad you're still with us to rib on me. But you had best put a sock – or maybe, a whole package of pantyhose – in that mouth of yours right now."

"Sorry, ma'am."

Rogen quieted herself down and looked at Delby with a less irate expression. "You know, if I could give out tickets for awful jokes, you'd have gone bankrupt paying off all the citations I would've given you by now."

The captain followed up that remark with a quick reassuring pat on Delby's shoulder, a move so atypical that it elicited a quick smile from the dour officer.

"Thank you, Captain."

"Okay, I want you to listen to me now. I have no doubt that you did the best you could to help your fellow officers tonight. I know that Bedowsky and Smith were friends of yours. But we were up against something very dangerous and really unexpected; something you don't get training for in the academy. They died as heroes, and thanks to you and them, we got two civilians to safety.

"It's always the civilians under our protection that come first, and everyone with a badge is aware of that. So, don't you dare go blaming yourself for anything that went down tonight, or I'll have to put you on report for unethical conduct against yourself. You hear me?"

"I do, Captain. Thank you twice."

Delby struggled to maintain her composure and succeeded. Only a single tear flowed down her left cheek to indicate the extreme distress she felt over witnessing the slaughter of three respected comrades – two of whom she considered to be friends – by a monster she never dreamed was part of the reality she knew.

Moments later, Rogen parked in front of the Calloway home and was let in by the detective assigned there, a bald, corpulent man with a thin moustache named Rodney Coogan.

"Captain," Detective Coogan said. "We have a situation here. I'm trying my best to keep Mr. and Mrs. Calloway calm."

"Wonderful," Rogen replied with consternation. "What is it now?"

"Their daughter fled the house when they weren't looking."

"That goddamned stupid girl!" the captain roared. "Why the holy hell would she do that when she knows what may be out there looking for her?"

"Her parents think she likely went to warn her friend Vance Jacobs. He's also a close friend of one of the murdered teens whom she believes to also be on the perp's 'hit list.'"

"Truly wonderful!" Rogen bitched. "We need to go looking for them now!"

"Captain Rogen," came Mrs. Calloway's voice from the entrance leading to the kitchen. "When my daughter has been scared or in a highly emotional state in the past, she would take refuge at the Marina Harbor, no matter what time of year it was. She thinks it's well-guarded and safe… but it may not be on a winter night like this. You… might want to check there."

"You heard the lady, Delby! Let's go!" the captain said. "I'll radio headquarters and while *en route* I'll request a SWAT team to meet us there!"

Mrs. Calloway sobbed but tried to remain hopeful as she watched the captain and her officer leave. Her husband put his arms around his wife for mutual support.

"Don't worry, babe," he said. "They'll find her. Our daughter is blessed. She always seems to have someone looking out for her. And I'll bet you that right now, someone is."

***

"We gotta keep moving, Vance," Kendra anxiously told her friend. "He shouldn't be able to see in this snowy wind any easier than us, but he can plow through the stuff on the ground lots faster."

"What was that thing that attacked the mummy?" Vance queried as he stumbled alongside the girl, partly supported by her shoulder. "Was it some big ass dog? Maybe it'll kill the mummy."

"I… I think it might have been that wolfman we heard about. I don't know why it showed up to attack the mummy, maybe a territory thing? I don't know and don't care, but we can't count on the wolfman killing the mummy."

"Where can we go? There ain't no police station around here. And we know we can't go to my house!"

"I don't know, Vance. My house will have a police officer stationed there, but a regular cop won't stop the mummy; and it will kill us and my whole family long before any back-up the policeman calls for can arrive."

"Where did that stupid friend of yours go?"

"You mean, Mike? I dunno, he probably ran off to get away from the mummy. Maybe he'll get some help, but we can't be sure. We need to take the short-cut to the Marina. The harbor is closed for the winter, but I know how to get in. It should still have security there that can call for help quickly."

Get up, Nero…

I had to force myself back to my feet. In this form, it would be my choice whether that would constitute two or four legs. I decided on the latter since I could move faster that way.

My bulky and powerful lupine body hurt in numerous places, particularly around the rib cage, but I seemed to heal a bit faster while unconscious, much like normal people do while sleeping. If I were going to help Kendra through this, I knew I had to move as quickly as I could despite the pain. I had her scent, and the noxious spoor of the mummy that Walt's mind now inhabited was too difficult to avoid even if I wanted to.

And… did I actually want to avoid it? I had to confess that this was the first time since becoming a werewolf that I got so thoroughly thrashed. There were hints before that I wasn't invincible, but this was the full confirmation of that unpleasant fact. In this form, I was one powerful mother fucker, but I could still get my shaggy ass handed to me by certain opposition. I highly doubted that the mummy was the only such entity out there with that capability.

I also didn't know if I could take this any further with Walt, because the truth was, I sympathized with him more than I did with Vance and Edwin. And he and I could indeed have accomplished wondrous things at each other's side if we pooled our power; maybe even create some kind of "Monster Squad"[3] or some shit like that.

But… he wanted to hurt Kendra. She was nice to me. She had a type of decency and level of tolerance that other people, both good and bad, were rarely inclined to show me. I knew that I was a jerk and an asshole; I was really bitter and emotionally scarred. Because of that, my tendency to "act out" made me a difficult person to deal with much of the time. But she was tolerant of me even on the worst of her days.

Also, while my dominant human side was terrified of facing down a foe as tough as the mummy again, the wolf aspect of my psyche feared very few things; it was fueled by animalistic fury rather than human-like emotions. It wanted me to lash out, to maim in retaliation for being injured. I had to decide on a course of action.

I'm sorry, Walt. I really am. But… though I may understand you and find you to be a sort of spiritual kin, Kendra is a better person than either of us. She is what we could have been if things had gone down differently in our lives; or, maybe if we had been born in another time and place with different values. And, frankly, the world needs more people like her and less of them like us.

I sped out of the alley and ploughed through the snow of the darkened city streets, following three distinct scents. My instinctual sense of direction soon made it clear that I was heading for the Marine Harbor, a favorite haunt of mine in both of my forms. Few people were out and about on this cold and snowy evening, which provided an advantage to both me and Walt. It was now only a matter of which of us would reach Kendra and Vance first.

---

[3] Hey, this was a few years before that name would end up taken, so no demerit points against Nero for that! Also, I just could not resist that homage! – the omniscient author

Kendra and Edwin finally climbed over a small metal gate that ineffectively blocked off the Marina Harbor for the winter season. They ran by the blacked-out, shack-like building that served as an ice cream shop during the summer.

With only a minimum of electric lights activated anywhere in the Marina during the cold winter nights, the icy environment provided a macabre ambiance. It was eerily quiet with dark, non-operational buildings scattered about. The lake was largely frozen over, and a gusty mist was tossed off the ice by the wind to create a weird atmospheric effect not unlike one seen in the forests from those classic Universal horror films.

In short, it looked like the perfect place for something strange and horrifying to take place. Worst of all, Kendra and Vance seemed to be the only two people there. They both scanned the area but saw no sentries or lighted security posts.

"Kendra, there's no guards here," Vance said as he continued to rub his now swollen throat. "You sure this was a good idea?"

"There *should* be a few guards here tonight!" she retorted. "Look around, and see if you can spot one walking around, or one of their stations set up somewhere."

"How the fuck can I see a person or some station through this fucking snow? It's blowing all over the fucking place like a big fucking blanket of white!"

"Stop complaining and look around! We should be able to see the glare of a flashlight if one of the guards is doing his rounds, or if we can spot any building that looks to be lighted from the inside."

"Kendra… Vance…"

"Jesus fuck!" Vance said through a pain-wracked larynx. "That sounded like *cough*… like it went into my head, not my ears!"

Kendra had no difficulty recognizing the ominous telepathic communique, though. "God, no… it's Walt. He's here, in the Marina."

"Aw, shit…"

The two turned to see the extremely tall outline of a powerfully built, yet repulsively gaunt humanoid form standing within the swirling mass of snow. The white whirl was due to the winds blowing sleet off the roof of a nearby vacant hot dog shop, and the giant form looked both majestic and terrifying while enveloped in its shimmery folds.

"Oh, god, no…" Kendra muttered as if her life was now measured in mere seconds.

Your mind directs the fetid mummy under your control to step out of the swirling winter snow, Walter Lavelle. This time your leathery black lips are pulled back in what resembles a fiendish grin. As you notice the look of abject horror on Kendra's face you take grim satisfaction in knowing that this frightening visage would be the last thing she would ever see before you ripped her limb from limb.

"Walt, please stop!" Kendra yelled to you over the blowing wind. "I didn't mean to hurt you! I'm sorry I didn't know how to deal with you properly. And I know that Vance was mean to you sometimes, but he's not a bad person. We can work this out. Please!"

"Do not allow that girl to manipulate you into going soft in the mind!" Nebka's consciousness shouts into your psyche with a burst of psionic force. *"She will only try to hurt and betray you again if she should regain the emotional upper hand!"*

I'm not stupid, Nebka. I know that!

"It's too late, Kendra," you "say" back to the girl you once considered a princess. *"You had your chance. Step away from that poltroon and maybe I will find a reason to let you live."*

"I'm sorry, Walt," Kendra whimpered, "but I can't just stand aside and let you do this. You... can't harm Vance without harming me too."

Vance's defiant attitude allowed him but one response: "Fuck you, Walt, you faggot! You're still a nerd; still a fucking *nothing!*"

"Vance, shut up!" Kendra screams.

"No!" Vance rejoins. "Fuck that pussy, needing a walking corpse to be a bad ass!"

"Like you thought you were when you picked on the weaker, Vance?" you psychically project into the injured jock's mind.

"Vance, please stop!" Kendra pleads to her friend. "Can you turn that damned ego of yours off for just one fucking minute? I can talk to him!"

"Fuck no, Kendra!" Vance exclaims. "Nothing you say is gonna stop him! So, let 'im kill us! I'm not gonna beg for my life to that asshole!"

"Then kindly be quiet so I do not have to listen to your big mouth as I rip you apart one piece at a time," was your psychic response as you plod toward the two helpless humans standing before you.

Instead of watching you tear their limbs off, however, the hapless duo instead witness the mummy taking a nosedive into the snow as a werewolf leaps onto your back like a ton of bricks.

"End... of the line, Walt," I told him.

"Fuck! The wolfman's back!" Vance exclaimed.

"And... it talked?" Kendra wondered aloud. "It... knows Walt?"

"Now it's my turn to tell you that we need to get the fuck out of here, Kendra!" Vance retorted. "Before one of them comes after us next!"

The two of them did their best to run as I tore into the mummy's back, hoping to rip out a vital organ; or failing that, as many of those wrappings as I could. Unfortunately, there seemed to be several layers of them, they were quite thick, and they appeared to have hardened and tightened over long centuries in the tomb. Still, I had him on his stomach, and I needed to keep him there until I could do some major damage.

"Damn you, Mike! Damn you to Hell!"

Before I could rip off enough material from the mummy's back to debilitate it, Walt made an interesting move. He twisted his right arm backwards, bent it at the elbow joint so that the forearm wrapped around my neck, and then he snapped it back so as to flip me off him (that's the best that I can describe it!). I had never seen a move like that before, and it stunned me as much as the physical impact of hitting the ground.

"That was an example of one of the many combat moves I learned during my original life," Nebka communicated to Walt. *"It is from a martial system likely not practiced or even remembered in this world of yours, acquired from an otherworldly race of hawk men who once interacted with my civilization. I was able to share it with you by taking more direct control of this body during a moment of hysterics on your part. Now, finish that foolish beast like you're worthy of my legacy!"*

I was back on my feet – two legs, this time – at the very moment Walt was. I was used to towering over most people in lupine form, but the mummy stood a few inches higher than me, actually surpassing seven feet. It added a bit of an intimidation factor to what his tremendous strength and resilience already provided.

I realized that my one hope of winning this duel of the monsters was to cut that rag-covered monstrosity into as many pieces as possible, and as quickly as I could, while avoiding those jackhammer fists of his. It was a tall order against a very tall opponent, but still my main option as I had no access to any source of flame in this cold, wet environment (I learned from the movies that mummies obviously did not like fire, as if common sense didn't tell you that!). In the meantime, the psychic link he established with me enabled us to continue "speaking" to each other telepathically.

"It sucks that you're making me do this, Walt!" I mentally griped.

With a growl of fury I rushed at him on two legs and tore a pair of large gashes in his bandaged torso with two quick swipes of my talons. I managed to do enough damage to send the mummy reeling for a few seconds.

"Damn you, Mike!" he responded. *"This is on you, you stupid, treacherous fool!"*

I then ducked under the first punch he threw at me and leapt away from the second – in each case avoiding blows that would have sent me flying. I dashed behind him on all fours and leapt on his back again, with one of my muscular furry arms wrapped around his neck in a vice-like grip.

"I'm sorry, Walt! But I can't let you hurt Kendra! You're taking this too far!"

"Hypocrite!"

I then wrenched his withered head upwards and tore open his throat with the talons of my free hand, ripping four long dark gashes into the rotten flesh. No blood flowed from the wounds, only a few puffy torrents of dust. So, I was evidently doing damage of some sort to the ancient vessel that Walt now inhabited.

"I said, you took it too far, Walt! We never had to hurt good people! Only the bad!"

The mummy let out another raspy hack as he grabbed the wrist of my clinging limb in a monstrously strong grip. Then he began pulling at it in an attempt to wrest it from his neck. I did my best to hold tight, despite knowing it was a struggle I was ultimately going to lose. I quickly decided to double down and wrapped my other arm around his throat. Then I pulled with all my might in an effort to tear the mummy's head from its body.

"Mike, you son of a bitch! We shouldn't be trying to destroy each other!"

"I have no choice, Walt! This has to end!"

The mummy countered by clutching each of my lower forearms with his long, steely fingers in an effort to wring both my arms from his neck before I could succeed in the intended decapitation. Thus, began a fierce tug-of-war that I was determined, but less likely than he, to win.

It was then that I could detect the sound of a police siren in the distance. Several dozen feet ahead of us, the fleeing Kendra and Vance also heard it. The cherry red flashing light at the top of the squad car quickly started illuminating the area around the Marina's front entrance a fluorescent vermillion.

"The cops are here!" Kendra shouted to the weakened friend she was helping to escape. "We need to turn and go back in that direction."

"You gotta be shittin' me, girl!" Vance replied. "Those two monsters are still fighting over there! What if the mummy won the fight and it's after us again?"

"I don't know! But still, we have to risk it! The mummy will likely be too distracted with the fight to get us!"

"Not a good idea!"

"We have to, Vance! The cops are there! They'll be another distraction for the mummy, and it will only take one of them to get us out of there! Let's turn back, now!"

Obviously, the person in charge of the situation faced by the fleeing duo, Kendra turned and pulled her injured friend back with her. They trekked across the snow as fast as they could, struggling not to slip and risk further injury, and they were soon approaching a spot several feet in front of where I was fighting the mummy.

Bad luck then descended upon them. As they were just two dozen feet from passing us the mummy finally won the tug-of-war when I could no longer match-and-counter his level of force. As he wrenched my arms free of his neck Walt pulled me off his back and slammed me onto the concrete.

The thin layer of snow covering the ground barely stifled the impact, so I was severely dazed. What saved me from a potentially game-ending barrage of pummeling was the mummy spotting Kendra and Vance running past us to reach the police near the harbor's entrance.

No! They won't get away! Walt decided as he lifted one of those big chunks of ice you often find on the ground in the Queen City during its winter season.

The mummy hurled the ice chunk at the two running humans, and it struck Vance on the side of his upper ribs with significant force. The thick winter coat he wore only slightly blunted the impact of the makeshift projectile. Vance screamed in agony and stumbled to the ground, his hand covering the painful spot where a rib had been fractured.

"Vance!" Kendra screamed. "Oh my god! You've gotta get up!"

"I can't..." he insisted as the side of his body burned with waves of searing pain.

"You have to! It's only a few more feet to the entrance..."

It was too late, however. The mummy charged at the duo and would be on top of them in seconds. As dazed as I was, I still managed to grab his rancid ankle and hold it as tightly as I could. That would have held almost any human being, but the mummy was far stronger than that.

He quickly pulled free of my grip, so I barely bought them an extra second of time. The bandaged fiend grabbed Kendra and Vance with each hand and lifted both screaming teens off the ground in a quick swipe of motion.

Kendra! No...

The mummy's next undoubtedly grisly move was abruptly interrupted by a flurry of bullets penetrating his head and chest. That was the first time I saw both Captain Jean Rogen and Officer Sharon Delby, as both ran into view with their guns drawn. The first barrage rattled the mummy with the unanticipated force of impact but failed to injure him or cause him to drop his hapless victims.

"He's still got them, Captain!" Delby noted.

"I'm gonna try something!" the captain shouted back.

Rogen slid down on one knee close to the mummy and fired a shot directly behind his knee at point blank range. It was an unexpected move that caused the joint to seriously buckle. The mummy likewise went down on one knee, this time dropping Kendra and Vance as the captain had hoped.

"Delby, get those civilians to the car! I'll delay this fucker until the SWAT team arrives!"

The officer grudgingly but unhesitatingly followed orders, understanding from the captain's earlier spiel that civilians under their protection must always come first.

"Follow me to the car! Now!" Delby yelled at the two.

"Vance is really hurt!" Kendra replied. "He can't make it on his own!"

"Then help me get him there!" the cop demanded. "Get your shoulder under his left arm, and I'll take the right!"

Kendra did as commanded, and the two women helped the pain-wracked, stumbling, and coughing Vance Jacobs towards the entrance of the Marina.

Now it was up to Rogen to do as she said until that damn SWAT team arrived.

The captain pointed her still-smoking firearm at the mummy as he stood up again, more or less completely shrugging off the kneecapping.

"Stay where you are, Mr. Lavelle!" she said. "Yes, I know it's you controlling that horrible bag of toilet paper! Give it up, a SWAT team is on its way! They'll pump you with enough bullets to tear that walking corpse you call a body to shreds!"

The mummy glared at her as Walt projected a psychic message directly into her mind, from which he also gleaned her identity.

"You have assured your own death by getting in my way twice in one night… Captain Rogen, is it?"

"Fuck you, rags!"

She fired two more ineffective slugs into the mummy until her gun began clicking to indicate the barrel was empty. The captain then swiftly holstered the piece and drew her nightstick.

"Are you serious, *Captain?"*

"I'm dead serious, asshole."

"No. You are simply dead!"

The mummy raised his piledriver fist, the captain barely wincing as she held her ground.

Before the unequal confrontation could proceed to its inevitable end, however, the mummy was knocked aside as I barreled into him again. I snarled viciously as I relentlessly ripped and tore at his wrappings and exposed shriveled facial skin with tooth and nail. He responded by pummeling at me furiously, causing no end of serious contusions and fractures all over my supernaturally enhanced form. We rolled about in the many inches of snow blanketing the ground, both of us determined to deliver the killing blows to the other.

As the mummy twirled about in his latest effort to extricate my savage self from his ragged person, we soon ended up a dozen feet away from the captain. We headed unerringly towards the metal railings that blocked off the sidewalk from the deep frigid waters of Lake Erie.

Moments later Delby ran back to Rogen's side.

"Captain, I called for back-up and a car took the civilians to the hospital," she reported.

"Good work," Rogen replied, "but why didn't you head there with them?"

"I wasn't going to leave you to face that thing solo, ma'am. I want several pieces of that bastard for myself too, to put a more selfish spin on things."

"Yeah, yeah. I should have ordered you to go with them, but I had to be hasty. Any sign of the SWAT team yet?"

"No, ma'am."

"Shit."

"Yea, I know. What should we do in the meantime?"

"Well, I'm out of ammo and my billy club won't do jack against those two, so I suppose we just sit on our assess and watch the free show. We'll do our best to keep the location secured until the SWAT unit arrives."

My fight with the mummy continued, both of us tearing and pounding at each other with savage fury. Once we were just a few feet from the rails the severe pounding I received took its toll on me faster than the many rips and tears I inflicted in turn. With my rapidly weakened state becoming evident, the mummy grabbed me and easily hefted me over his head with both arms. As my jaws were pulled from his face, a big chunk of his rotten dermis was torn from his right cheek and hung flapping like a strip of blackened parchment from my fanged muzzle. I spit the putrid shit along with a spray of blood from my mouth; that blood was unfortunately my own, as the mummy didn't bleed.

Walt then carried me the few feet remaining to the edge of the water.

"It's over for you, Mike! This is what you get for betraying someone who should have been a friend!"

He tossed me over, but I was quick to grasp his bandaged head in my hand immediately after he did so.

"Then it's not over for me alone, Walt!"

"Mike, you stupid bastard!"

As intended, my tight grip and the very inertia of my flung body helped to carry the mummy over the railing with me. We landed a dozen feet down on a thin icy sheathe covering the water. It cracked in several places under our combined weight. Both of us would be going down in the freezing drink within seconds but I was determined to avoid this fate by getting into position to perform a springing leap back up to the rails.

"No, you don't, Mike!"

I wouldn't make it as the mummy grabbed the upper and lower portion of my muzzle in each hand before I could execute the leap. He then pulled me down and began yanking my chops apart, clearly intending to snap my jawbone. I resisted with my great maw strength, but Walt was determined, and the bones were already beginning to crack.

I knew I had to act *fast,* and the animal-like reaction time I possessed in lupine form enabled me to do exactly that. I pushed myself upwards and enacted a reverse-headbutt to the mummy's sternum as hard as I could muster.

The blow both dislodged the mummy's hold on my muzzle and caused him to slip and fall backwards on the ice. His heavy body landed with a loud thud and cracked the sheathe beneath us completely. We both fell into the freezing depths of the lake and began sinking fast. The mummy desperately grabbed my wolf-like ankle as we went under.

"Why, Mike? Why did you do this?" Walt projected into my mind. *"We should have been friends, you idiot! We could have taken the world together!"*

"I wish we could have, Walt," I replied mentally as our link began to fade. *"I wanted that! But... you crossed a line..."*

I frantically kicked at his vice-like grip with my free leg several times, until I finally managed to extricate my ankle. I obviously couldn't breathe underwater, and the below zero temp was beginning to become too much even for my heavy natural coat and supernatural metabolism to endure. I didn't know how to swim either, but I waved my mighty arms to direct myself upwards towards the surface, hoping my effort would pay off before either the lack of air or the extreme chill would take its toll.

The mummy's body, however, was too heavy and seemed to suffer from negative buoyancy. It continued to sink deep down into the depths of Lake Erie's cold winter waters.

"Nebka!" Walt mentally called out to the consciousness of the long-dead pharaoh with great urgency as the bandaged form they co-habited sank further and further. *"What should I do? Help me!"*

"There is nothing that can be done now, you foolish whelp!" was Nebka's solemn response. *"You failed me! Failed* us..."

As Nebka's psyche drifted into full dormancy, Walt's own consciousness was in a state of utter panic as the mummy continued to sink further and further down.

Dear gods, what can I do? If I make the exchange here, I'll die immediately. What can I do? What can I dooooo...?

No answer came as the mummy, with Walt's psyche trapped inside, plummeted further and further down into the freezing darkness of the lake.

Meanwhile, back up on the surface, Rogen and Delby watched the two of us sink below the waves and pondered their next move as they still awaited the arrival of the SWAT unit.

"They both went under, ma'am!" the officer said. "Neither re-surfaced! Do you think...?"

"What I think," Rogen replied, "is that I'm not sure if either of them can actually die that way, at least not as we understand the term. The mummy may not need to breathe and may not be affected by the cold, but a body that size is probably going to sink right to the bottom. It may be that Walter Lavelle's mind is stuck in it, as I have no idea yet as to how he controlled the damn thing. That would be a horrible fate for the kid, but what can you do?"

"As for the werewolf, I imagine he can't breathe underwater and I'm not sure how immune to the cold his furry ass is, but..."

A second later both were startled as my "furry ass" leapt out of the water and grasped the metal rail just as the last remains of the icy sheathe broke under me. I then pulled myself up with one mighty heave and was back on the snowy concrete, just a few yards from where Rogen and Delby were standing.

I instinctively shook a bunch of water off my coat in the manner of a true canine. The two lawwomen covered their faces to avoid their facial skin and eyes being spattered by the freezing droplets. I then sensed their presence, turned in their direction, and growled in preparation for trouble.

"Captain...?"

"Keep your hand on your gun but don't draw and shoot unless he comes at us."

Once I realized they were not going to try and shoot me unless I made a move against them first, I turned around and dashed in the opposite direction at high speed. I quickly disappeared from their line of sight to be swallowed up by the blowing wisps of snow on the horizon.

***

"So, it would seem Middleton was right," Rogen said as she and Delby watched the huge canine figure disappear into the distance. "There really is a werewolf on the loose. Both a werewolf and a mummy turned up in Buffalo? And then there was that situation with the Jack Dog a month ago. What the hell is it with this city? At least we can scratch the mummy along with the Jack Dog off our list of concerns. But in the future what type of bizarre headache for us is going to pop up in their place?"

"Since I can't answer that question and would hate to ponder it anyway, ma'am," Delby responded, "why didn't you want us to open fire on the werewolf when it jumped out of the lake? We could have maybe scratched that concern off our list as well."

"It just… didn't feel right, for some reason. That creature prevented the mummy from killing both those two civilians and the two of us by its intervention. I figured there is possibly more to it than we understand, and that maybe it earned a reprieve for this one night. And according to reports, it also helped to end the threat of the Jack Pack."

"But Middleton already said it's dangerous, ma'am. It injured him and his partner, and it also attacked and hurt several civilians."

"Yes, I know that. So, I understand we can't just ignore its presence in the city. I have plans for that which I'm going to put into motion as soon as we check up on Billington and the other civilians whom we got to safety today."

The two lawwomen then turned around as they heard the multiple footsteps of the SWAT team stampeding into the harbor.

"Now they show up," Rogen said with an eye roll.

The black-attired, heavily armed and armored unit swiftly surrounded the area, their riot guns out and ready to fire.

"Captain Rogen!" the leader of the unit said as he recognized her. "What's the situation?"

"Unfortunately, you missed all the excitement, Commander Boulder. It's all taken care of; the civilians were safely spirited away, and Delby and I are still among both the living and the anatomically intact. Speaking of which, mister, your squad really has to improve its response time!"

Before Boulder could reply with one of his usual hot-headed comments, Rogen received a sudden dispatch call from her Kord Tech walkie-talkie.

"Yeah, what is it, Coltrane?" she asked the officer on the scene at the museum.

"Captain," Coltrane squawked in, "if you're not otherwise occupied, you've gotta get yourself here to the museum ASAP! Immediately, if you can! You really gotta see what we just found here!"

***

About twenty minutes later Rogen entered the museum where she met Coltrane and his assisting officer Decker at the Egyptian exhibit.

"It's right over here, Captain," Coltrane said as he led Rogen to Nebka's sarcophagus. "Decker and I were performing a thorough search of the premises with a focus on this exhibit as per your orders. When we opened this whatever-you-call-it casket, instead of the mummy that's supposed to be in there we found, um… him."

Rogen looked into the ancient tomb to find the catatonic but still living body of young Walter Lavelle, his arms crossed over his chest and his eyes tightly closed. He was wearing his bifocals, winter jacket, and gloves.

"Dear god," she said. "That, I believe, would be Walter Lavelle. The *real* Walter Lavelle, whose mind, I imagine, is now trapped at the bottom of the drink inside the mummy's body."

"Say what, Captain?"

"Never mind. It'll be in the report that you're going to have some serious trouble believing. Have this kid's body brought down to the juvenile prison infirmary for medical evaluation. And I want him watched under constant guard no matter how long he stays in that coma! In the meantime, I have the dubious honor of reporting this to his father."

***

"My son is… in a coma, you say?" was Bradley Lavelle's query into the phone as he spoke with Captain Rogen. He had heard her clearly the first time, but his state of mind forced him to request clarification.

"Yes, Mr. Lavelle, that is correct," the captain replied as gently as a hardened veteran like her was capable. "We… found him laid up in the sarcophagus – did I pronounce that right? – of the mummy exhibit in the museum. You're aware he was working as an intern there, correct?"

"Yes… I am aware."

"Okay, I just had to check to be certain. As it seems your son must have been secretive about a lot of things with you, Mr. Lavelle."

"I… don't disagree with you, Captain. I know how he was. But can you tell me exactly what you mean in this case?"

"It's a complicated story, Mr. Lavelle, and I need to discuss things with Commissioner Langston before I can give you the full story."

"Captain, Walter is my son! I want you to tell me what happened to him and what he was up to! What went on in that museum that got him put in a coma and stuck in that mummy casket? I know it has something to do with that goddamned museum!"

"It does, Mr. Lavelle. But as I said, it's a bit complicated to explain over the phone, and before I get it down into words with a full report. Right now, you should go to Buffalo General and be with your son. The doctors will tell you about his overall condition when you get there. In the meantime, wait for my call and I'll have you come to the station to give you my full report on… what might have caused all of this."

"You better! Or I'm gonna sue both the Buffalo police and that fucking museum! *Both of you!* I'll sue the whole goddamned city if I have to!"

"I understand that you're upset right now, Mr. Lavelle. So, go to the hospital to be with your son. I'm sorry to have had to tell you this, and I'll be in touch very soon."

As Captain Rogen hung up, Bradley Lavelle slammed the handset of the phone down almost hard enough to smash the device. He then slumped down on the sofa and mournfully buried his face in his hands as he struggled to contemplate how this could have happened, and exactly what part his parenting may have played in the bizarrely tragic turn that his son's life had taken.

***

It was now once again well past 8 PM in the evening, and Mike Nero still had yet to return home. It went without saying that his mother, stepfather, and grandparents were all worried and very pissed off… but more of the latter at this point in time due to the recurring nature of the situation. That was the state of mind his grandfather James Nero Sr. was in when he answered the atypically late ringing of his back doorbell.

The irate, shortish, but strongly-willed and strongly-built middle-aged man opened the door to see his grandson's sometime friend Marcus Gekko standing there. The man's already bad mood was in no way improved by the sight of a neighborhood kid he was not exactly fond of.

"Hi, Mr. Nero," Marcus said a bit nervously. "I'm sorry to come here so late, but it's important."

"What do you want, Marcus?" James demanded to know. "Mike isn't home yet!"

"I know, sir, and that's why I came here now. I… have to talk to you about your grandson."

"What? Is he into that gang shit again, or into drugs, or…?"

"No, no, sir. What he's into is a lot worse than anything like that. And I need to let you know about it. Can we talk for a minute?"

***

The next morning at the Niagara precinct station where Captain Rogen operated, Officer Lamar Middleton sat chatting with fellow patrolman Lenny Cantor. The latter was in charge of gathering reports of wolfman sightings, and as usual, Lamar was eager to hear them.

"It's cool that you were granted your request to get off sick leave early, Lamar," Lenny said.

"Captain Rogen helped with that," Lamar replied. "That's why I'm in this room here. She wanted to speak to me about something, and for some reason she wanted you here for it too. Anyway, until she arrives, I'd like to know if there have been more sightings."

"Yeah, and some of them are a real trip! There was a very recent report that a guy claimed to have the wolfman attack him in the restroom of a Doublemeat Palace while the dude was taking a piss! Hah hah! You can't possibly believe all this shit, Lamar? This wolfman mania is bigger than Beatle Mania! At this point I wouldn't have been surprised if that guy had claimed that the wolfman offered to hold his dick for him as he peed. I'm not sure if that incident really happened, but it would've been hilarious if it did! Hah hah hah!"

"Let me tell you something, Lenny. Or, rather, show you something. You may find that story funny, and the guy who reported it may or may not be making it up but trust me… that werewolf is no joke. It's injured several people already, and it did this to me a few days ago."

The officer pulled up a sleeve on the casual shirt he wore to reveal the ugly, still-healing scars that the werewolf's nails had ripped into his upper bicep.

"Oh, man, Lamar. I'm sorry. I didn't mean to be insensitive…"

"Sure you didn't, Cantor," came Rogen's voice as she entered the room, immediately drawing both Lamar and Lenny to firm attention. "And that brings us to why you're here now, Middleton, and why I want Cantor, our wolfman archivist, to be present too.

"I saw your werewolf the other night during an incident at the Marina Harbor. You can read the full report later."

"Jesus, Captain," Lamar said. "Did it attack you? Did you manage to shoot it?"

"Neither of the two," the captain replied, "and in fact, it's a rather complicated story, as you'll see when you read the full report. For now, however, let's say that I realize there is indeed a werewolf, or at least something very much like one, loose in the Queen City. I understand that it can be very dangerous to civilians.

"I further agree that it must be contained or stopped in some manner. To that end, due to your multiple experiences with it and your fine showing during the Jack Dog incident, I spoke with the commissioner and the mayor last night, and they both agreed to a proposal of mine.

"As of this morning, you will be promoted to the rank of Sergeant and put in charge of a special task force whose main purpose is to track down this werewolf and see to its containment or... neutralization, as mentioned above. And also, as needed, to deal with some of the other strange things popping up lately in the city.

"Cantor, you're on the task force as official archivist. This special unit is to be directly answerable to me, and me to the deputy commissioner."

"Cool!" Lenny replied with his usual child-like zeal.

"Wow, thank you, ma'am," Lamar said as he got over the initial surprise. "This is an honor, Captain! I will give you my best work and I promise to fulfill the purpose of this task force, now that I can devote myself full time on the matter. You have my word on that."

"I'm sure I do, *Sergeant* Middleton," the captain replied. "But don't thank me for it, nor should you consider it an honor rather than a burden. I got a good look at some of the strange things now appearing in the Queen City last night, and the werewolf may just be the tip of the iceberg. I don't envy you this job, and I can only hope that you and the other officers assigned to your task force will all survive to collect your pensions.

"Still, I would seriously suggest opening a very big life insurance policy for your families."

END

Nero Book 3: Season of the Witch Sisters **should be coming your way during the first week of April 2021! Watch for it, or Nero will bite yo' ass!**

If you liked what you just read, please do not be shy about leaving a positive review on Amazon, Goodreads, your personal blogs, etc., as the more of that we get, the more of Nero and other great projects Wild Hunt Press can bring you at very affordable prices! This author is always striving to improve his craft, so that my number of hits will greatly outweigh my misses.

If you are seeking more of Mike Nero, then look for his present-day exploits, where he is a monster hunter code-named Beowolf, in the following upcoming volumes from Wild Hunt Press. Short stories and novellas featuring contemporary exploits of Nero will appear in every volume of our forthcoming monster hunter anthology *Boogey Knights*; and every volume of WHP's forthcoming horror series anthology *Mansion of the Macabre* will feature Mike Nero stories that take place in the various years since he became an adult. And yes, if the *Nero* series continues in popularity, you can look forward to a series of *Beowolf* novellas and novels! The sky is the limit with your support, and we are honored to receive it!

ABOUT THE AUTHOR

Christofer Nigro is a lifelong fan of the horror genre, as well as kindred genres such as sci-fi, fantasy, super-heroes, kaiju, pulp adventure, and crime noir. His interest in these genres also covers just about all mediums, including prose, comic books, RPGs, cinema, TV, and video games. He writes in all these genres as well, and has been a published author since 2010, making his debut in Black Coat Press's annual French pulp anthology *Tales of the Shadowmen*. Since then, he has had short stories, flash fiction, novellas, and novels published by Pro Se Press, Sirens Call Publications, Horrified Press, Grinning Skull Press, Severed Press and others before going on to found Wild Hunt Press, so he could pursue these genres in his own inimitable style. He writes and edits full time, is a cat person, is heavily into social activism, and enjoys fine food and pleasant weather.